FULL OF BEANS

More Novels by Jennifer L. Holm

The Fourteenth Goldfish

Eighth Grade Is Making Me Sick

Turtle in Paradise

Penny from Heaven

The Boston Jane series

The May Amelia books

Also by Jennifer L. Holm and Matthew Holm

Sunny Side Up

The Babymouse series

The Squish series

My First Comics Series

The Comics Squad series (with Jarrett J. Krosoczka)

FULL OF BEANS

JENNIFER L. HOLM

Random House New York

Text copyright © 2016 by Jennifer L. Holm
Jacket art copyright © 2016 by The Little Friends of Printmaking
Jacket lettering by Jaclyn Reyes

Photo credits: pp. 181, 182, 184 courtesy of State Archives of Florida;
p. 185 John Kobal Foundation/Moviepix/Getty Images.

Visit us on the Web! randomhousekids.com

Educators and librarians, for a variety of teaching tools, visit us at RHTeachersLibrarians.com

Library of Congress Cataloging-in-Publication Data
Names: Holm, Jennifer L., author.
Title: Full of Beans / Jennifer L. Holm.
Description: First edition. | New York : Random House, [2016] | Companion to Turtle in paradise.
| Summary: Ten-year-old Beans Curry, a member of the Keepsies, the best marble-playing gang in Depression-era Key West, Florida, engages in various schemes to earn money while "New Dealers" from Washington, D.C., arrive to turn run-down Key West into a tourist resort.
Identifiers: LCCN 2015041078 | ISBN 978-0-553-51036-2 (hardback) |
ISBN 978-0-553-51039-3 (ebook) | ISBN 978-0-553-51037-9 (lib. bdg.)
Subjects: | CYAC: Moneymaking projects—Fiction. | Gangs—Fiction. | Key West (Fla.)—
History—20th century—Fiction. | Depressions—1929—Fiction. |
BISAC: JUVENILE FICTION / Historical / United States / 20th Century. | JUVENILE FICTION / Social Issues / Friendship. | JUVENILE FICTION / People & Places / United States / General.
Classification: LCC PZ7.H732226 Fu 2016 | DDC [Fic]—dc23

Printed in the United States of America
10 9 8 7 6 5 4 3 2 1

First Edition

Random House Children's Books supports the First Amendment and celebrates the right to read.

For Will, who wanted a story about Beans

CONTENTS

FULL OF BEANS

Key West is semi-tropical; it has never known a frost: The winter season is practically devoid of rain. There is no smoke, soot, or dust to mar the beauty which nature has lavished on this Island City. . . . Key West is an ideal vacation ground.
—Brochure produced by the Key West Administration to advertise Key West as a tourist destination during the Great Depression

LYING LIARS

JULY 1934

Look here, Mac. I'm gonna give it to you straight: grown-ups lie.

Sure, they like to say that kids make things up and that we don't tell the truth. But they're the lying liars.

Take President Roosevelt. He's been saying on the radio that the economy was improving, when anyone with two eyes could see the only thing getting better was my mother's ability to patch holes in pants. Not that she had a choice. There was no money for new threads with Poppy out of work. It was either that or let us go naked.

Then there was Winky. He was the lyingest liar of them all.

"You said twenty cans for a dime, Winky!" I pointed at the small red wagon.

It was full of empty condensed-milk cans. I found them for Winky and cleaned them up. Even smoothed the sharp edges. Winky sold the cans to Pepe's Café, where they used them to serve *café con leche*—espresso and condensed milk. Everyone in Key West drank leche, even toddlers.

"You must have wax in your ears, Beans," Winky replied. He had a potbelly and slicked-back, greasy hair that matched his slippery ways. The armpits of his Cuban-style shirt were stained yellow. "I said *fifty* cans."

I was so burned up by his words that steam just about burst out of my ears. And believe me, it was sweltering outside. Key West in July was stinking hot.

Especially stinking.

Garbage had been piling up ever since the town ran out of money to pay for collecting it. Flies swarmed above the rotting mounds. They were filthy and disgusting, and my brother and I had spent the entire morning in them.

Me and Kermit had dug through steaming piles of

garbage from one side of Key West to the other, looking for milk cans. We'd dodged stray dogs and mosquitoes and fearless rats. I couldn't imagine a worse job in the whole world. Except maybe cleaning outhouses.

Now Winky was trying to cheat us out of our money?

"I heard you just fine," I told him. "You said *twenty*."

"Sorry, but you're full of beans, Beans," Winky said, and then laughed. "Look: I made a joke. Get it? *Full of beans?*"

"Hilarious," I said, and glared. "You're a regular comedian, Winky."

"I suppose I could give you a nickel for twenty," Winky offered us, like he was a king doing us a favor.

"A nickel?" I wasn't very good at arithmetic, but even I knew that this was a lousy deal.

"Sorry, Beans," Winky added with a smirk. "Maybe you can find someone else to sell the cans to?"

I glared at him. I would if I could, but everyone knew that Winky had the only milk can game in town. He was a cousin of Pepe's.

"Beans," Kermit whined, tugging on my shirt. "I'm hungry."

I sighed and rolled my eyes. Kermit wore crooked glasses and couldn't drive a bargain with a kitten.

Winky saw the advantage and took it. A fake kindly expression lit up his face. "Why, Beans. Your little brother's hungry. I bet a nickel would buy a nice lunch."

I swallowed my pride.

"Fine," I muttered. "We'll take the nickel."

"What's that?" Winky asked loudly. "I didn't quite hear you."

I glared at him.

"I said we'll take the nickel!"

He dropped the coin into my outstretched palm.

"C'mon, Kermit," I snapped. "Let's go."

As we walked away, Winky shouted, "Always a pleasure doing business with you, Beans!"

I'd been Winkied again.

We sat in the shade of a sapodilla tree, eating our lunch. Broadcasts from radios tuned to Havana stations drifted out open windows. The streets were deserted. Everyone took siestas to avoid the worst heat of the day. Key West at noon was sleepy.

"That's the last time we work for him," I muttered.

"You say that every time, Beans," Kermit said, munching on the measly lunch the nickel had bought us: cracker sandwiches. Crackers with a smear of mustard and a tiny bit of ham.

I'd wanted to buy a real ham sandwich from Pepe's Café. They made it Cuban-style—ham, mustard, cheese, and pickles, toasted on fresh Cuban bread. It was delicious.

"Well, this time I *mean* it," I vowed.

"Aw, he's not that bad," Kermit replied. "He gave us a nickel!"

"We earned a *dime*, Kermit."

Kermit was only eight and didn't understand how life worked. Maybe when he got to be ten, like me, he'd smarten up.

"Gee, do you think if we collect fifty cans for Winky tomorrow, he'll give us another nickel?" Kermit asked.

Then again, maybe not.

"I'm still hungry," Kermit complained.

"Get some dilly gum," I told him. The sap of the sapodilla tree made good chewing gum if you didn't much care about taste.

Kermit scraped back some bark and dug out a wad of the sticky sap. Then he started chewing. Getting it soft took a while. Even though it was free, it still took work.

A rumbling motor had my ears pricking up. There weren't many cars in Key West; even the folks who owned them couldn't afford gas.

The shiny automobile rolled down the dirt road, hitting every gaping pothole. It looked strange and out of place, like something from a Hollywood picture.

Kermit gave a low whistle. "That's some ride!"

"It's a Ford Model 730 Deluxe V-8 sedan," I told him. I'd recognized it immediately from the newsreels. "The same car that Bonnie and Clyde drove."

Everyone knew about the dead outlaws.

Kermit looked at me. "You think a criminal is driving that car, Beans?"

The car slid to a stop and parked across from us, and a man climbed out.

"I doubt it," I said. I couldn't imagine any criminal who walked around without trousers.

Kermit's eyes bugged out behind his glasses. "Is he just wearing his underpants?"

"Sure looks that way."

The underpants in question were long; they hit him just above the knee. They showed off pasty-white, hairy legs. On top, the portly man sported a long-sleeved suit shirt with a bow tie. He finished off the whole ensemble with a fedora. Maybe he was someone's relative who had just gotten out of the loony bin. Wouldn't be the first time.

He wrinkled his nose and looked around.

"My, that certainly is a powerful smell," he said, walking over to us. He had a thick mustache, and from the way he spoke, I could tell he was from off the rock. A stranger.

"You should smell *us*, mister!" Kermit exclaimed. "We been in that garbage all morning!"

The fella looked us up and down, from our bare feet to our patched-up pants. "Yes, it seems you have. Who might you young gentlemen be?"

"I'm Kermit!" Kermit was like the mayor of Key West. Kid would talk to anybody. "This is my brother Beans!"

"How quaint," he murmured.

I narrowed my eyes at him. "Did you just insult us?"

"Of course not, young fella. Why, I'm here to help you." He held out his hand. "I'm Julius Stone, Jr. Pleasure to make your acquaintance."

I stared at the outstretched hand but didn't take it.

When someone says they're gonna help you, they're just waiting to stick their hand in your pocket and take your last penny. I should know. I got relatives.

"Mister," I said, "you're the one that needs help. You ain't got no pants."

He looked offended. "They're supposed to look like this! They're called Bermuda shorts. They're the latest fashion."

At loony bins, no doubt.

"So, tell me, Peas . . . ," he began.

Peas? Maybe he was deaf in addition to being crazy.

"Is the rest of the town in a similar state?" he asked. He waved his hands at the weathered gray wooden houses, set close together, that lined the street.

"What do you mean?" I asked him.

"Are all the houses this decrepit?"

"Huh?"

"Run-down," he said bluntly. "Unpainted. Falling over. Crumbling. Et cetera."

"I guess," I said with a shrug. Most folks in Key West were on relief. Paint was a luxury. Our town looked like a tired black-and-white movie.

The man frowned.

"Where you from, mister?" Kermit asked.

"Why, I've come all the way from Washington, D.C. I've been sent here by President Roosevelt himself!"

Yep. Definitely a lunatic.

"Sure, the president sent you," I said, and laughed.

Mr. Stone looked offended. "You don't believe me?"

"'Course I believe you, mister," I said. "Why, we just had the Queen of England visit here last week."

"I'm not lying!"

But I just shook my head. "Whatever you say, mister."

Like I said: grown-ups are lying liars.

LITTLE PESTS

Key West was lousy with lanes.

There were dozens and dozens of them. Some had funny names like Stump Lane and Donkey Milk Lane. Then there were the ones named after the big Conch families that settled on them when they first came from the Bahamas: Sawyers Lane and Higgs Lane and Thompson Lane.

We lived in a little Conch house on Curry Lane. Where else would we live? We were Currys.

Our place was shotgun-style, one and a half stories. We rented it from some shirttail cousin on my father's side. My mother said he should have paid *us* to live in it, because the place was full of pests. Termites. Ants. Roaches. Scorpions. But the worst pest in the joint was still in diapers.

Buddy.

My mother was wrestling my three-year-old baby brother into the crib in his little bedroom upstairs. He was squirming and rolling around and rubbing his eyes.

"You need to go down for a nap right this instant, Buddy," my mother told him.

"Noooo nap!" he howled, red-cheeked. "I don't wanna!"

"Hiya, Ma," I said.

My mother wore her hair neat and tidy in a bun. Her dress was always pressed. Sometimes I thought it was my mother's will alone that kept the house from collapsing around us.

She took a whiff and wrinkled her nose. "*What* is that smell? Have you been in the garbage again?"

"We were getting cans," I said. I held out the penny I hadn't spent from our nickel.

Her face softened and she shook her head. "You're a good boy, Beans. But you keep that."

I slipped it back in my pocket.

Then she sighed and stared at Buddy. "What am I going to do with you, child?"

I started to back away slowly. I knew where this was going, and it was nowhere good.

"Beans," she said.

I froze and watched as she plucked a squirming Buddy out of his crib and held him out to me.

"Take Buddy out. I can't get any washing done with this one in my hair." My mother took in laundry for other families in town to help pay the bills.

"Aw, Ma, do we have to?" I asked, eyeing my dangling baby brother with distaste.

She practically threw him at me.

"Go," my mother said, adding, "Maybe he'll nap for you."

Buddy just howled.

Our bare feet kicked up dirt as Kermit and I walked down the lane, pulling Buddy in the wagon. We were shoeless, like every other kid in Key West, and didn't care.

Kermit looked back and whispered, "He's following us, Beans!"

The dog had been trailing after us for a while. More of these dogs than ever before were roaming around, and they were thin and gaunt and fearless. This one had a little body and a roundish head and reminded me of Popeye's girlfriend, Olive Oyl.

"He's probably just hungry," I said.

The dog had a lot of company. All around the country, folks were having hard times. I'd heard stories of people lining up overnight just to get a bowl of soup. Here in Key West, we had it better than most. There was a whole ocean with fish and lobsters to catch. Not to mention all the fruit trees. Just about the only thing that didn't grow on trees was money.

"You think he'll eat us?" Kermit asked with alarm.

"He'd have to be pretty desperate to want to eat Buddy," I said.

Buddy had been crying since we left. He'd cried all the way down Curry Lane. Down Frances Street. Down Fleming Street. Now we were at Grinnell and he was still howling. He was tired from not napping, and he'd be mean as a mosquito by suppertime if he didn't sleep. I'd had enough.

"Go to sleep, Buddy," I told him.

"I don't wanna!" he howled. "I'm a big boy!"

"You're annoying, is what you are. Now go to sleep right this minute or I'll box your ears."

He yelped and covered his ears. He knew I would.

"Lie down," I ordered him, and he settled into the wagon. Before he could protest, I tucked the blanket around him tight, flipping it over his head.

We started walking, and in no time flat, Buddy was fast asleep. The lulling movement, combined with the heat, had knocked him out like a prizefighter's punch. Worked every time.

Kermit shook his head in amazement. "Maybe we should tell Ma about that trick."

"Don't be a dummy. Then we'd have to watch him every day."

Fishing boats were pulling in at the waterfront, their decks flopping with the day's catch.

We passed the turtle kraals, the pens at the dock where they kept giant sea turtles like a herd of cows.

Turtle was good, cheap meat. 'Specially for stew. Fishermen caught the turtles out at sea and brought them turned on their shell. A turned turtle couldn't flip back over. I always wondered what it felt like for the turtles to be dropped into those kraals.

Down the way, I recognized one boat in particular: it belonged to Johnny Cakes. Rumor had it that he was involved in all sorts of criminal enterprises, although he'd never been arrested. People said you could get away with anything in Key West, even murder. I thought the rumors were because of Johnny Cakes's flair for fashion. Today he was wearing a white linen suit and a Panama hat.

His sharp duds weren't the only thing that set Johnny Cakes apart from the other fishermen at the docks. There was also his cargo. It wasn't exactly flopping.

There were three coffins stacked on the deck.

"Who died?" Kermit asked.

Johnny Cakes took off his hat and waved it. "Terrible malaria epidemic in Havana. These poor fishermen got caught up in it, I'm afraid," he said. "I'd just dropped off my cargo, so I volunteered to bring them home so their families here can see them on their way."

"Golly! You sure are a Good Samaritan!" Kermit said. "You'll get into heaven for sure."

Johnny Cakes's mouth twitched.

The blanket in the wagon moved as Buddy rolled in his sleep.

Johnny Cakes cast a curious look at our wagon. "What've you kids got in that wagon? Kittens?"

I shook my head. "Baby."

Just then, Buddy woke up and whimpered. His hand knocked off the blanket, so I flipped it back over his face.

"Aren't you being kind of hard on the tyke?" Johnny Cakes asked me.

"You've gotta be hard to handle bad babies," I told him.

The best sight in the world greeted us when we returned home: our father's worn, muddy shoes sitting on the front porch.

Poppy had been chasing jobs up the Keys for the last few weeks. He said looking for work was more worry than a hard day's labor. Everything felt wrinkled to us when he was gone. Ma was crankier and Buddy seemed to cry more.

Poppy looked tired and dirty, but I didn't care. I just threw myself in his arms and breathed him in. His whiskers were long and scraped my cheek.

"Poppy!"

"Did you grow?" he teased. It was what he always asked me.

"Just my hair," I said.

Supper was conch chowder. Conch was easy to harvest from the ocean. Poppy's father had been a conch fisherman, like many others who had left the Bahamas to settle in the lanes of Key West. That's why we were called Conchs. We ate conch chowder all the time, but for some reason it tasted better than ever. Probably because Poppy was home.

After supper, we kids washed the dishes while Poppy tended to my mother's hands. They were red and raw from the harsh detergent she used to do the laundry.

Poppy mixed some cornstarch and water into a gluey paste. Then he smeared it gently onto my mother's hands.

"That feels so much better," she said.

He gave her a kiss on the forehead.

"That's why you married a Curry boy," he said.

"Humph," Ma replied.

All of a sudden, a loud bell started ringing.

Kermit looked excited. "Fire bell!"

Most of the houses in Key West were made of wood and built close together. When a fire spread, it could take down a whole lane. There was a tall fire bell in the cemetery, which alerted everyone.

"Is it nearby, Poppy?" Kermit asked.

Poppy pulled down the fire alarm card. Every house

had one. The number of rings indicated the location of the alarm box.

"Count it out," Poppy told us.

I listened carefully to the ringing.

"It's one-three-four!" I looked down at the card. "Eaton and White Streets!"

"I was gonna say that, too. You always beat me!" Kermit groused.

"Beans is just older than you. He knows more," my father told him.

"Someday I'll know more!"

I snickered. "Not likely."

"That's enough excitement for one night. Off to bed with you children," Ma said.

Kermit and I shared a tiny, hot bedroom.

I'd papered the walls with funny pages from the newspapers. My favorite was *Little Orphan Annie*, the strip about an orphan girl named Annie who gets adopted by a bald millionaire named Daddy Warbucks. I didn't care much for Annie. I wanted to be Daddy Warbucks when I grew up and live in a fancy mansion. Or at least have my own bedroom. I hated sharing a room with Kermit. The kid snored.

After we were settled in bed, I couldn't sleep. The smell of kerosene lingered in the air. My mother burned rags soaked in the stuff to smoke out the mosquitoes when they got thick. They were thick as a rug tonight.

But it wasn't just the smell and the pests. My heart was still beating fast from the rush of the fire bell. Kermit didn't have any such problem getting to slumber land. The kid could sleep through a hurricane.

My father's voice drifted up a crack in the floorboards.

"Up north, New Jersey," he said.

"Where will you stay?" my mother asked.

"Mildred's place. Ernest swears he can get me a steady job at the factory, with good wages."

"But it's so far," she murmured.

"Maybe we can all go?" my father said.

"How? We don't have the money to make the trip. Besides, do you really think your sister wants five of us coming to live with her?"

I could almost see her shaking her head.

My father sighed unhappily. "All right, then. I'll go up first. See if I can get work. Then I'll send for you and the boys. Move the whole family there."

"Let's be sure to leave my mother here," she joked.

But I didn't see anything funny about it. My stomach was churning. Move to New Jersey? I couldn't imagine living anywhere but Key West! It was the only home I'd ever known. Everything—and everyone—I knew was here.

"Should we tell the children?" Ma asked.

"Not until I have something sorted out," my father said.

After that, their voices lowered, and I lay awake in the dark, worry about the future buzzing like a mosquito in my head.

I didn't fall asleep until the sun was coming up.

Poppy left for New Jersey two days later.

"Are we gonna have to move away?" I asked him.

He hesitated, then said, "Of course not."

But I knew he was lying. Just like every other grown-up.

As he walked down the steps with his sack thrown over his shoulder, he ruffled my hair.

"Keep an eye on your mother and the little ones," he told me. "You're the man of the house now."

Buddy started crying before Poppy even reached the end of the lane.

KEEPSIES

At Pork Chop's house on Ashe Street, people were always coming and going. The Soldanos had a telephone, and not many other people did. The phone rang all day long with calls for neighbors. It was a party line, which meant everyone who had a phone could listen in on conversations. Ma said the gossipy Conchs loved the party line.

The other reason for all the traffic at my best pal's house was that Mrs. Soldano sold *bolita* numbers. Bolita was a Cuban lottery game. Everyone in Key West was crazy for it.

But I didn't come for the phone or the bolita: I came for the cooking. Mrs. Soldano made the best food in the world, Cuban specialties like *arroz con pollo* (chicken and rice), garbanzo soup, and *flan* (egg custard).

"Here you go, boys," Mrs. Soldano said as she set a big plate of *bollos* in front of us.

Bollos were ball-shaped fritters made of black-eyed peas deep-fried in oil. They were garlicky and spicy and made you toot. My favorite.

"Thanks, Mrs. Soldano," I said.

"*De nada*, Beans," she said with a smile.

"Thanks, Mami," Pork Chop said.

Pork Chop had been my best pal since our bungys were in diapers. He knew all my secrets and I knew his.

"Oooh," Kermit said, picking up a bollo, then putting it down. He picked up another one, inspecting it.

"Don't touch every single one of them with your grubby fingers!" Ira said.

Ira had a mop of curly red hair and was like a boy version of Little Orphan Annie. He was another member of our gang, which included me, Pork Chop, and Kermit. It wasn't my idea to include Kermit, but I couldn't get rid of him because he was my brother and I had to watch him anyway.

"I can't decide which one to eat," Kermit said, his hand hovering over the plate.

"For the love of Pete, Kermit! Just take one already!" Pork Chop ordered.

Kermit grabbed one and started eating.

"I hear there's gonna be a game this morning," Ira said.

Marble fever was gripping Key West, and we were the best crew on the island. We called ourselves the Keepsies because we won so many other kids' marbles. Our pouches held every kind of marble imaginable. We had them all: cat's-eyes, aggies, clearies, milkies, steelies, glassies, onionskins.

"Who's playing?" I asked.

"The Mighty Mibsters."

They were a marble crew from Stump Lane. "Mibster" was what you called a marble player. They thought they were being clever with their name.

"Word is, they're saying they can beat us," Ira added with a look.

Pork Chop scoffed.

"Baloney!" he said. Pork Chop had a way with words.

Ira nodded. "They're just high on their horse after beating those Caroline Street kids."

"What are we waiting for?" I asked, pushing back my chair and slapping on my cap. "Let's go win some marbles."

As we walked down the street, Kermit kept looking behind us.

"He's following us again!" he whispered loudly.

"Who's following us?" Pork Chop asked.

"Termite!"

Sure enough, the funny-looking dog was behind us. He was impossible to get rid of, which was why we'd started calling him "Termite."

But he wasn't the only pest around. We'd just passed the fire alarm on the corner of Frances and Fleming Streets when a towheaded kid in overalls, with no shirt on underneath, waved to us from the front step of his house.

"Hey, fellas!" he trilled.

I groaned. It was Too Bad.

"Want to play marbles?" Too Bad asked, holding up a fabric pouch.

The kid's real name was Marvin. But in the Key West tradition of nicknaming, everyone called him Too

Bad because he was terrible at marbles. We only let him play with us when we were bored and felt like beating somebody. He wanted to be in our gang. Every single kid wanted to be in our gang.

"We're busy, Too Bad," I said.

"Too bad, Too Bad," Pork Chop added.

But the kid wasn't easy to brush off. If the dog was a termite, Too Bad was a flea.

"What're you doing? Where you going?" he shouted after us.

"Mind your own potatoes!" Pork Chop told him.

His face fell.

"All right, then. See ya later, pals!" Too Bad called after us, waving wildly.

Stump Lane was one of the unofficial marble courts. The dirt was good and it didn't get muddy, which was important. Couldn't play marbles in mud.

I heard kids whispering as we walked up.

"Here comes Beans!"

"It's the Keepsies!"

"They're undefeated!"

It was music to my ears. Marbles were where it

was at: a kid could make himself a reputation as a good marble player. No one got all that excited about flying a kite.

The Mighty Mibsters were waiting for us. But they wouldn't have to wait long to lose. Nobody beat the Keepsies.

We had a winning strategy. Pork Chop came in strong and scared 'em by taking hard shots. Then Ira knocked them off balance by picking off marbles at the edge. Finally, I did cleanup by knocking the farthest ones out.

We won three games in a row and a whole bag of marbles.

I turned to Pork Chop. "Guess those Mibsters ain't so mighty after all, huh?"

"You shred it, wheat," Pork Chop said.

A girl walked up to us. She had freckles and wore her hair in soft waves like the Hollywood actresses these days. Her name was Dot, and she was the best girl marble player on the island.

I hated her.

Dot dangled out her bag of marbles. "Want to play, Beans?"

"I'm done for the day," I said. "Won three times."

"Why? You scared?"

"We don't play girls." It was as simple as that.

"I'm good enough to be in your gang," she said, jutting her chin out.

"No girls allowed in the Keepsies," I said.

"I'll play ya, Dot!" Kermit offered happily.

"For the love of Pete, Kermit!" Pork Chop said in disgust. "You can't play her! Don't you know anything?"

I could have told Pork Chop that Kermit didn't.

"Come on, fellas," I said, and we started walking.

I heard Dot shout, "I'm going to beat you one of these days, Beans Curry!"

CUT-UP

Me and the gang were sitting on Duval Street, watching our toenails grow.

Duval Street was where all the action happened—not that there was a whole lot of that these days. The Casa Marina Hotel was closed, and most of the other businesses were boarded up. But my two favorite places were still open. The first was El Anon. It sold the best ice cream on the island. Every flavor imaginable—sugar apple, tamarind, soursop, guava, mango, coconut. The second was the movie theater. There was a picture playing called *Baby, Take a Bow*. It starred a kid named Shirley Temple.

I loved the pictures. I loved everything about them. The music. The scenery. Most of all, I wanted to *be* in pictures.

Hollywood was a place where kids like us were making it Big, with a capital B. Jackie Cooper. Spanky McFarland. Wheezer Hutchins. Dickie Moore. My favorite star was Baby LeRoy. The kid was just a baby and he was a movie star! He even had a studio contract with Paramount.

A bunch of kids came strolling down the street, hawking Spanish limes. They had a little song and everything:

> *We got limes!*
> *Get 'em sweet!*
> *Like a piece of turkey meat!*

Everyone was a salesman in this town. There was a fella who sold flopping fish straight out of a wheelbarrow. Another man sold handmade lollipops. Still another sold eggs from a basket, and another sold coconuts.

Pork Chop stared at the kids selling the limes. "That's a good racket."

It gave me an idea.

"Maybe that's what we need to do," I told the gang. "Peddle something."

"What?" Ira asked.

"I know!" Kermit said. "We can sell gum!"

"Gum?" I asked.

"It's free. We just have to dig it out of the dilly trees," Kermit said.

"Probably should add some sugar," Pork Chop said. Then he looked at me. "What do you think, palsy?"

It was a good idea. Everybody liked gum. Well, except my uncle Dewey, who didn't have any teeth.

"Gum it is."

We got down to business the next day. But it turned out that making gum for a lot of people was harder than just making it for yourself. First of all, you couldn't get much sap out of a single sapodilla tree, so we had to crisscross town, scouring streets for dilly trees.

After nearly a whole morning, all we had was a

half-filled cup of tacky gum. But that wasn't the only problem. We had to get the sugar into the gum, but it was too sticky to stir with a spoon.

"I give up," Pork Chop said, after trying to mix in the sugar.

"Just chew it," I said.

"Chew it and then sell it to people?" Ira asked.

"Sure. It'll get nice and soft. Not like they're gonna know, right?"

We took turns chewing chunks into small balls. Then we wrapped them in wax paper and started hawking them.

"Fresh gum!" we called. "A penny apiece!"

All afternoon, we walked back and forth across Key West, trying to sell our gum.

We didn't sell a single piece.

"Some hot idea that was," I said as we stared at our basket of unsold gum.

"What do we do with it?" Ira asked.

"Give it to Too Bad, for all I care," I said.

So he did.

Too Bad even thanked him.

• • •

It was the dairyman who gave me the hot idea.

The man had a walking dairy. He sold milk door-to-door to housewives, straight from a cow. The fella was the smartest peddler in town, in my opinion. He sold something folks needed, and he went right to the customer.

It made me think. What was something that everyone needed? It seemed that in lean times like these, you didn't actually need much. Kids ran barefoot all over Key West, and we didn't care one bit that we didn't have shoes.

The answer fell in my lap. Or, rather, on the *ground*.

We were roaming the lanes, looking for a game of marbles, when we passed a house with a big mango tree out front. There were ripe mangoes all over the ground underneath the tree.

"That's it," I said. "We'll sell fruit."

"Like the kids that sell the Spanish limes?" Pork Chop asked.

"Nah," I said. "We're gonna sell it as lunch. We'll cut it up and sell cups of it to the fishermen down at the docks. Everyone needs lunch."

"Not bad," he said.

The first thing we needed to do was gather fruit.

We scoured our own backyards, but all we came up with was one mango, a Spanish lime, and a soursop.

"We're gonna need a lot more fruit than this," I said.

"What do you expect us to do?" Ira asked. "Just go into people's yards and steal fruit off trees?"

"Why not?" I asked.

"I don't know about this, Beans," Ira said.

"We won't get in trouble if it's *already* on the ground," I told him. It was an unwritten rule that if the fruit was on the ground, it was okay to take—even if it was in someone's yard.

Ira didn't look convinced.

"Don't worry," I assured him. "We won't be the ones picking it up."

"So you're saying I just have to climb the trees and shake the fruit so it falls down, and then bring it to you?" Too Bad asked me.

"Don't get caught," I added.

"Do I get to be in your gang?"

"Let's see how this goes first."

His eyes widened in understanding. "It's a test, right?"

"Exactly," I said.

The fellas and I sat around playing marbles.

Too Bad returned a few hours later.

"Here ya go, Boss!" he said, and held out a basket full of fruit.

The kid was annoying. But he was kind of growing on me.

I knew better than to bring a bunch of kids into the house when Ma was ironing, so we went over to Too Bad's.

His mother wasn't home. As we walked through the front door, I spotted a fire key hanging on a hook. Folks who lived near the fire alarm boxes had keys to set off the alarm. It was considered a big responsibility.

We got to work cutting up the fruit in the kitchen. After it was all cut, we mixed it up in a big bowl. I took a taste.

"It needs something," I said, looking around the kitchen. Then I saw it. Old Sour—key lime juice preserved with salt. Every Conch had a bottle of it in their house.

I added some Old Sour, with a dash of salt for good measure, and stirred. Then I took a bite. It was sweet but tangy.

"Perfect!" I declared.

We poured half into another bowl and grabbed some cups. We left the rest in the icebox to chill and headed to the docks.

They were crowded with fishermen working their boats. We started peddling. I even made up a little ditty to sing:

> *Fresh fruit cut-up!*
> *It's the best!*
> *So tasty and delicious,*
> *You can't resist!*

Slow Poke, a sponger, was our first customer.

"What've you got there, kids?" he asked us, wiping his sweaty brow.

"Fresh fruit cut-up," I said.

"How much is it?" Slow Poke asked.

"A nickel a cup."

"Not a bad deal on a hot day like this," he said. He fished in his pocket and pulled out a nickel.

Ira served him a cup of cut-up.

"It's good, kid," he said. "Kinda refreshing."

After that, all the men on the docks started buying from us. We were selling out fast.

"Too Bad!" I shouted. "Go back and get the rest. Quick!"

An hour later, our bowl was empty and Too Bad was nowhere in sight.

"Where is that kid?" I asked Pork Chop.

"Got me," he said.

I was about to send Ira looking for Too Bad when we saw him coming up the way, carrying the other bowl.

"Shake a leg!" I called. "We got customers!"

He handed me the bowl. It was empty.

"Where's the cut-up?" I asked him.

"I couldn't resist, Beans," Too Bad said.

"You ate it? *All* of it?"

His mouth turned into a sad frown. "It was just so tasty!"

"You can forget about being in the gang," I told him.

"I don't feel so good," Too Bad said, and clutched his stomach. Then he opened his mouth.

And puked all over my feet.

That's when I changed my mind. Too Bad was the most annoying kid in the world.

BUM DEAL

Even though Too Bad had eaten (and thrown up) some of our profits, we'd made enough to buy us all a ticket to the pictures. Except for Too Bad, of course. We were using his share to buy popcorn.

The sun was setting when Kermit and I went to meet the gang on Duval Street for the early show. We passed Jelly, on his way home. Jelly was a wiry-looking older man with graying hair.

"Hi, Jelly!" Kermit greeted him. "You going home for supper?"

Key West was so broke that they let the inmates go

home for supper because it was cheaper. Jelly was in jail for passing bad bills.

"You better believe it," he said.

"We're going to the pictures!" Kermit said excitedly. "The new Shirley Temple movie!"

"Well, have fun, kids," he said with a wave.

As we neared the movie theater, we saw a thick crowd forming outside Pepe's Café on Duval Street.

"Look, Beans!" Kermit said, pointing. "It's the lunatic!"

Sure enough, Mr. Stone was standing in the center of the throng in his underpants. Right away, it was clear that he was no kind of salesman. Judging from the shouts, no one was buying whatever he was peddling. They were riled up.

"Good people of Key West," Mr. Stone shouted. "This is a grave situation. Your city is bankrupt. Your streets are littered and filthy. Your homes are run-down and your industry is gone. Something must be done!"

"Who made you boss?" someone hollered.

A man next to me grumbled, "He's one of them Roosevelt New Dealers!"

"The governor has appointed me as administrator,"

Mr. Stone told the crowd. "The management of this town has been turned over to the federal government."

Someone shouted, "Is that even legal?"

Kermit turned to me. "I thought he said the president sent him here."

"What do you expect? He's a lunatic," I replied.

"We must think of the future! We must clean up and rebuild!" Mr. Stone said.

"Build what? A factory?" a woman up front asked.

"Not a factory," Mr. Stone said quickly. "You see, I have carefully studied the options, and I believe that we can turn Key West into a tourist resort!"

Stunned silence met his announcement. Then someone laughed.

"A tourist resort?" a mustached man scoffed.

He was our resident writer. Apparently, he was famous. I'd started to read one of his books, but I couldn't get past the second page.

"Time is of the essence!" Mr. Stone said. "The first season will start in December."

"Who's going to pay for all this?" a man asked.

Mr. Stone gave an awkward smile. "There are federal funds set aside to pay for supplies, but all the work must be done on a volunteer basis."

"You mean you ain't gonna pay us?" someone shouted.

"You want us to work for free?"

"That's a bum deal!"

Then everyone was shouting and hollering.

I shook my head. This Stone fella was worse than Winky.

And that was saying something.

We beat the rest of the fellas to the movie theater. I recognized the skinny man behind the ticket window. His real name was Mr. Peacon, but everyone called him Bring Back My Hammer. He'd gotten his nickname because someone was always borrowing his hammer and he was always yelling at them to bring it back.

"How's the new picture?" I asked him.

"Better than most," he said.

Kermit whimpered behind me. "Beans . . ."

"Is she as good as Baby LeRoy?" I asked.

"Better," he said. "This Shirley Temple kid's gonna be a star."

"Beans!" Kermit hissed.

I looked back in annoyance. "What's the matter with you?"

He squirmed a little. "The thing is, Beans . . ."

Then he scratched his bungy.

I couldn't believe it. "Again?"

His face crumpled in misery.

"I got worms," he whispered.

Just like that, my dream of going to the pictures disappeared in a bottle of Bumstead's Worm Syrup.

The ringing bell on the door of Gardner's Pharmacy sounded like money disappearing from my pocket. The store was open into the early evening, like many places in town.

"Well, hello there, Beans, Kermit," Mr. Gardner said. "What can I do for you?"

I jerked my head at my brother. "He's got worms again."

He gave Kermit an appraising look.

"Ah, I see," he said. "I have just the thing."

The pharmacist went into the back, returned with a little glass bottle, and handed it to me. It was etched with the words *Bumstead's Worm Syrup.*

"That'll be twenty cents, Beans," Mr. Gardner said.

I could barely make myself hand over our picture money, but I did.

"Hope you feel better, Kermit," Mr. Gardner called after us.

When we got back to the movie theater, Pork Chop and Ira were waiting for us.

"Where you been? Show's about to start," Pork Chop said.

"We ain't going in," I said.

"What? Why?" he demanded.

I thumbed at Kermit. "Because we spent our money on his bungy. He's got worms again."

Ira exclaimed, "Again? You're the wormiest kid in Key West, Kermit!"

Kermit's lip started to quiver, and his eyes welled with tears.

"Aw, don't go having kittens!" Pork Chop said.

"Let's go home," I told my little brother.

I dropped off Kermit and his Bumstead's at the house and told Ma I was gonna go for a walk. Truth was, I just wanted to get away from Kermit. I couldn't bear to be around his wormy self after what had happened.

Talk about a bum deal.

Termite waddled after me as I walked down the

dark lane. The electric company had turned off the streetlamps long ago when the city couldn't pay its bills.

Up the way was a bar where fishermen liked to hang out. Key West was a thirsty town. Nothing could shut down the bars and taverns. Not Prohibition. Not even this Depression.

Johnny Cakes was sitting by himself at a little table outside, smoking a cigarette.

"Ah, just the young man I wanted to see," he said, his face illuminated by candlelight.

I was shocked. "You were looking for me?"

"Yes." He tilted his head. "Are you interested in a job?"

"Do I have to do anything dirty?" I asked suspiciously.

"That depends on what you consider dirty," he replied.

"Do I have to dig through garbage?"

He barked a laugh. "No garbage, I promise you that."

I lowered my voice. "Is it something *illegal*?"

Johnny Cakes stared at me, cooler than the other

side of the pillow. "I'm an upstanding businessman. I would never be involved in illegal enterprises."

Then he blinked.

"Can I think about it?" I asked him.

Johnny Cakes waved a hand. "Thinking never helped anyone, kid."

Just then, I heard my name being called.

"Beans! Got any more cans for me?"

I looked into the bar. Winky was sitting on a stool, a sloppy look on his face. He was probably drinking my milk can money.

"That kid's my best worker," Winky confided loudly to the man sitting next to him. "He'll crawl through anything for me. And I do mean *anything.*"

Then he burst out laughing.

It wasn't right. Sure, I'd always been a good boy. Like Ma said. But I didn't want to be a good boy anymore. Good boys were suckers. They crawled through garbage. They got paid nickels instead of dimes. They didn't even get a lousy ice cream.

That was it. I wasn't going to be good anymore. From now on, I would be tough. I would be hard.

I would never be Winkied again.

I turned to Johnny Cakes.

"I'm done thinking," I told him. "I want the job."

"Wonderful. Come by my office tomorrow. Be sure to bring the wagon."

"Can Kermit come, too?" I asked. "I'm supposed to watch him during the day."

"Sure thing." He smirked. "But leave that baby at home."

So began my life of crime.

THE CRIMINAL LIFE

The neighborhood of Key West where the cigar factories were located was called Gatoville. Mr. Gato was the fella who had started the whole cigar village. Poppy says when he was growing up, it hummed with activity. But like just about every industry in Key West, it had disappeared. Now only a few folks made cigars. The big buildings that used to hold hundreds of workers sat empty. Johnny Cakes owned one of them.

I knocked on the door, and my new employer opened it a moment later.

"Hiya, Johnny Cakes!" Kermit waved.

"Come on in, kids," he said.

Kermit and I filed into the dark building. There were rows of benches and tables where the men and women used to roll the cigars, and it smelled faintly of tobacco. A pile of wooden cigar boxes was stacked in one corner.

We followed him up a flight of stairs, and then Johnny Cakes paused outside a door.

"Before I take you in, you must swear that you will not tell a single person what you are going to see."

"Uh—" I started to say when Kermit interrupted.

"I can keep a secret, Mr. Johnny Cakes! Why, I've never even told Ma that Beans uses Nana Philly's girdle to keep my baby brother from jumping out of the crib when he's supposed to be watching him. He just girdles Buddy right up to the bars! Baby can't escape! It's the—"

I covered Kermit's mouth. "We won't tell anyone."

Johnny Cakes seemed to take my measure for a moment and finally nodded. "This way."

When he opened the door, I couldn't stop the gasp that tumbled from my mouth.

The place was stacked with coffins! Dozens of them!

Was he secretly a murderer? Like the outlaws Bonnie and Clyde? What had I gotten us into?

"Look," I said quickly. "I don't think this is for us. But we won't tell a soul, I swear."

"Come pay your respects, boys," Johnny Cakes said, lifting the lid of one of the coffins. "They all died happy."

I shut my eyes quickly! I didn't want to see a dead body!

Or *did* I?

When I opened my eyes, there wasn't a corpse in sight.

The coffin was full of liquor bottles.

"Booze?" I asked.

Johnny Cakes grinned at me. "Cuba's finest."

"What about the dead fishermen? The malaria epidemic?" I demanded.

Johnny Cakes shrugged.

Did I mention that grown-ups are lying liars?

Johnny Cakes explained that, on principle, he refused to pay the government for a liquor license, which was why he was bringing in the liquor secretly.

"Principle?" I asked.

"It cuts into my profits," he said shortly.

"So what do you want us to do?"

He smiled slowly. "You, my sweet, innocent children, are going to deliver this precious cargo to the fine establishments of our fair city. In your charming wagon, of course."

"What if someone stops us?" I asked.

"Nobody's gonna stop a couple of kids pulling a wagon," Johnny Cakes said. He didn't look the least bit concerned. "Put the booze under a blanket. If they stop you, just tell them you got a sleeping baby under there."

I remembered my resolve to be hard and shoved my newspaper-boy cap low on my head.

"We don't work for less than a dime," I told Johnny Cakes.

"Each?" he questioned.

Kermit's eyes widened, and I looked at Johnny Cakes.

"Each," I said firmly.

"You drive a hard bargain. But I can respect that. I'm a businessman myself." He sounded impressed. "A dime it is. You'll earn it."

We huddled on the street with our wagon full of booze. It was packed tight under the blanket. Johnny Cakes had warned us darkly that he would take broken bottles out of our pay.

"I don't think this is a very good idea, Beans," Kermit said, looking around.

I was nervous, too. I was pretty sure my mother wouldn't be happy if I got my little brother arrested for rum-running. But this was my chance to get out from under Winky.

"It'll be fine," I told him with more calm than I felt. "We'll do like Johnny Cakes said. Act normal."

We pulled the wagon carefully down Duval Street. I was just turning into an alley to go to our first bar when I heard Kermit chattering behind me.

"Hiya, Mrs. Sweeting! How are you?"

"Why, hello there, Kermit! What are you boys up to?"

"Well, we're just pulling the wagon!"

"What's in the wagon?" the old lady asked.

"Oh, just some liq—"

I elbowed Kermit hard.

"Ow!" he yelped.

"Buddy's sleeping in the wagon, Mrs. Sweeting," I

said smoothly. "We gotta get him home to Ma. C'mon, Kermit!"

The minute we turned the corner, I rounded on him.

"What is wrong with you?" I demanded.

"I forgot about it being a secret!" he wailed.

"Don't talk to anybody else," I warned him.

"But, Beans," he said, "if I *don't* talk to folks, it will seem weird."

He had a point.

It turned out Kermit was our lucky charm. Not a single person gave us a second glance after Kermit opened his mouth.

All my worry turned out to be for nothing. Even the tavern keepers didn't seem surprised to see a couple of kids at their back doors with a wagon full of liquor. One of them even fed us lunch. It was the sweetest racket ever.

At the end of the afternoon, Johnny Cakes paid us each a dime.

"Good work, kids," he said.

A dime in my pocket and I didn't smell like garbage? If I'd known being a criminal was this easy, I would have been bad a long time ago.

INVASION

I was finally seeing the Shirley Temple picture. I was going to the late show by myself and had left Kermit at home. He'd spent all his Johnny Cakes money on ice cream from El Anon and had a bellyache.

The theater was mostly empty. I sat in the balcony. A man was already sitting there, and he was wearing a black fedora hat low over his face.

It was strange enough for a man to wear a hat inside; it was very rude, I knew. But something else about him sorta struck me as off. Then I realized what it was:

he was wearing gloves. I'd never seen a man wearing gloves. They gave him an old-fashioned look, like he was from another time.

But then the projector started rolling and I forgot all about the gloves. I was transported to a world where men wore shiny shoes, kids tap-danced, and ladies were called dames. It was nothing like the life I knew in the lanes of Key West.

Acting didn't even look that hard. All you had to do was pretend. I could do that. I just needed to get a screen test with Warner Brothers.

The picture was good. Shirley Temple stole the whole show. Boy, was Bring Back My Hammer right: this kid was gonna be a star.

Before I knew it, the credits were rolling. When the lights came up, the gloved man was gone, melted into the shadows. There was something on the ground by his chair: a wooden cane with a polished glass knob on top.

I stopped by the ticket booth and handed the cane to Bring Back My Hammer.

"The man in the balcony left this," I told him.

"What man?"

"The one with the gloves."

"I didn't let no man in with gloves," he said. "Maybe you saw a haint."

"Haint" was what Conchs called ghosts.

"If you say so," I said.

But something even more unbelievable than haints showed up the next morning.

I was in the outhouse, flipping through the Sears, Roebuck catalog. It came free, so we used the pages to wipe. They sold just about everything. Rubber tires. Ladies' brassieres. Typewriters. Bathtubs. Potato planters. Diamond rings. Anything you needed, you could find in these pages.

I loved imagining what I would buy from the catalog if I was rich. A sewing machine for Ma. A new pair of shoes for Poppy. A high chair for Buddy. A bicycle for Kermit. And for me?

I wanted an accordion.

An accordion seemed like something only a rich person would have. Because nobody needed an accordion. I imagined having a party and saying, "You want to see my accordion?" and watching every single kid's mouth drop open in amazement. I had the model all picked out and everything. I was even gonna get a fancy case.

My dreams were interrupted by the loud sound of a truck thundering down our quiet lane. I finished my business and walked into the house. Everyone was huddled around the front door, looking out.

"Did the circus come to town?" I asked.

"Better than the circus," my mother said. She opened the door so I could see out.

Men in the lane were shoveling garbage onto the bed of the truck. Termite barked at them.

"They're picking up garbage?" I asked.

"Apparently," she replied. "Will wonders never cease?"

Fast-talking men in Bermuda shorts started showing up everywhere. Key West was being invaded.

By New Dealers.

"There's another one!" Pork Chop said. We were walking down Frances Street when he pointed out a skinny man with white legs in Bermuda shorts.

"I hear the New Dealers took over a building downtown to organize the volunteers," Kermit piped up.

"Volunteers? You're all wet!" Pork Chop said.

"It's true!" Kermit insisted. "Folks are volunteering to help clean up!"

"What a bunch of applesauce!" Pork Chop said, shaking his head.

I couldn't agree more.

The New Dealers didn't appear to have a lick of sense. Especially the head lunatic. We ran into Mr. Stone on Grinnell Street. He was in his underpants—I mean, Bermuda shorts—as usual. He was standing outside a house with a bunch of other New Dealers in their underwear.

"My good man," Mr. Stone was saying to the old Conch man sitting on the porch, "you need to open the shutters on your house."

"Why?" the old man asked.

"Because we want Key West to look hospitable."

"The shutters keep the house cool," he replied.

"Sir, if you would just allow me to demonstrate what I'm talking about," Mr. Stone said.

The old man shook his head. "Have at it."

Mr. Stone walked over to the shutters and started to tug them open. They were stuck.

"Mister," I said, "you don't want to do that."

"I know exactly what I'm doing, Peas!" Mr. Stone huffed.

"It's Beans," I corrected him, but he just ignored me.

I knew the man was crazy, but it turned out he was dumb, too. Mr. Stone tugged the shutters open and then screamed, nearly falling over himself as he stumbled back.

A small black creature with claws and a waving tail scuttled up the side of the house.

"Was that—was that a *scorpion*?" Mr. Stone gasped, holding his hand to his chest.

"They like to nest behind the shutters," I said. "That's the *other* reason we keep 'em closed."

Later that afternoon, I saw another fella in Bermuda shorts. This one wasn't taking down shutters, though. He was painting a picture of them.

The fella had set up an easel in front of a little Conch house on Nassau Lane. I stopped to watch him paint. He'd copied the yard and house perfectly: the uneven wooden fence, the listing palm trees, the open scuttle window upstairs. But it was the colors that drew me in. In his version, the dull gray house had cheery yellow shutters, the brown of the palms was a fiery orange, the roof was a burnished red. The whole picture was bright and inviting like a movie poster, instead of looking like a tired old house hidden behind overgrown weeds.

He glanced at me. "What's your name, kid?"

"Beans."

"I'm Avery. Nice to meet you," he said. The man paused and puffed on his pipe. "So what do you think, Beans?"

"You're painting it all wrong," I told him.

The artist arched an eyebrow. "How so?"

"The house isn't yellow. All those other colors— they aren't there, either."

"I think you just need to look a little harder," he said, and winked.

His accent was strange. "Are you one of them New Dealers?"

"I suppose you could say that."

"What do you do?" I asked.

He waved his paintbrush at the canvas. "This."

"Paint pictures?"

"We're creating postcards and a brochure to advertise Key West as a tourist destination."

"Where'd you learn to paint?"

"Hollywood. I used to paint titles for the silent pictures."

"You were in Hollywood working in pictures and now you're painting houses? You sure must have done something wrong!"

He made a face. "It wasn't exactly in the plan, but then again, nothing ever is."

I watched him paint for a little bit.

"You need some people in there," I told him, pointing at the canvas.

He cocked his head.

"Otherwise it seems kind of dead. Who would want to visit a dead town?"

"Very astute observation," he said. "I think you might secretly be an artist."

"No way, no how," I said. "I want to be rich. I don't want to end up painting houses!"

BAD BABY

It was cool now, but it would be unbearable in a few short hours.

"Make sure you don't let anything fall off the wagon!" my mother called as we set off down the lane.

Our wagon didn't carry babies or booze that morning. It hauled trousers and slips and stockings. It was me and Kermit's job to deliver the laundry Ma washed around town.

We did our rounds: knocking on doors, dropping off bundles, and picking up the dirty clothes. Sometimes folks gave us a tip—a cookie or a piece of homemade candy. Kermit liked to linger and talk the ear off of the poor person who answered the door.

At the firehouse on Grinnell Street, Fire Station No. 3, the doors were wide open. The firemen were sitting around a table, playing dominoes.

"Who's winning?" Kermit asked them.

"Me." A heavyset man with no eyebrows gave a small smile.

"That's because you cheat, Cem," one of the other men grumbled.

Cem got his nickname because everyone said he should already be in the cemetery, on account of the dangerous work he did. This wasn't the first time he'd burned off his eyebrows.

"Hot enough for you?" I asked him.

It was our little joke. Cem liked to say that Key West in summer was hotter than some of the fires he'd been in.

I pulled out a bundle of clean undershirts and handed them to Cem.

"Thank your ma for us, will you?" Cem told me.

Ma took in some of their washing for free because the firefighters of Station No. 3 never closed their doors like the other firehouses did when their firefighters weren't getting paid. She said they were heroes.

"I will," I said.

The next house belonged to my favorite client of Ma's.

Mrs. Albury had apple cheeks and wore her chestnut hair in a bob like a Hollywood movie star. She would have been beautiful except for the big dark circles under her eyes. The red-faced, bawling baby in her arms was the one who gave them to her.

Little Dizzy.

"Hiya, Mrs. Albury!" Kermit said. "Hi, Dizzy!"

Mrs. Albury gave a weary smile. "Hello, boys."

"We brought your laundry," I said.

"Thank you, Beans," she said. "There's some fresh divinity in the tin by the sofa. Help yourself."

I didn't have to be told twice. Mrs. Albury made the best divinity candy in all of Key West. It was chocolate and sugar spun into sweet little dollops that melted in your mouth.

Dizzy cried louder.

"Dizzy's a little fussy today," Mrs. Albury said apologetically.

Fussy? I'd seen a lot of screaming babies in my time, but Little Dizzy took the top prize: shrieking, red-eyed, with feet kicking. The kid was a bad baby. No doubt about it.

"What's wrong with him?" I asked.

"He's got a terrible rash," she said, and lifted his long white cotton dress to show the baby's bungy. The skin was red and chapped and raw.

"Hmm," I said. "Can I go in your kitchen for a minute? I think I know something that may help."

"Sure," she told me.

I dug around in the cabinets while Kermit talked Mrs. Albury's ear off. I found a tin of cornstarch and shook some into a teacup, added a little water, and made it into a paste.

"Try this on Dizzy's bungy," I told her.

She looked at it dubiously. "What is it?"

"Secret formula. My mother uses it on her hands, and it always works," I told her.

She gave a shrug. "I'll try anything at this point."

When we left her house, the sun was burning high in the sky, and the air was so thick with humidity, we could barely breathe.

Our last stop was at a house where we didn't like to

linger. It belonged to Nana Philly. The meanest lady in Key West.

Nana Philly was notorious. She made grown men cry. She'd chased three pastors out of town. Folks whispered that she was so mean, she must be related to the devil himself. Black cats crossed the road just to get away from her.

We parked the wagon on the street, and I started to organize the bundle of clothes in a neat pile. Heaven forbid that the clothes had a wrinkle.

"I'm melting," Kermit complained.

"Go knock on the door," I told him. "The faster we deliver the laundry, the faster we can get in the shade."

He climbed the porch steps and knocked, looking back at me. "Maybe we can go take a dip in the ocean?"

Just then, the door banged open and a wave of water flew through the air, splashing onto Kermit.

Nana Philly stood there holding an empty bucket.

Kermit gasped like a fish, choking.

"What are you kids doing here?" she snapped.

"Delivering laundry," Kermit said weakly. He looked down at his shirt. There was a red-and-brown smear on it now. "What was in the bucket?"

"Dirty water from washing up. Maybe some blood and guts. I was butchering chickens for stew."

Kermit looked stricken. "Blood? Guts?"

"You shouldn't have gotten in the way. I was tossing it into the yard. Besides, what are you complaining about? At least the water cooled you off."

Did I mention that Nana Philly was also our grandmother?

"Uh, here's your laundry," I told her, passing it off. I grabbed Kermit's hand and tugged him behind me.

We started walking fast down the street, pulling the empty wagon.

"Where is my girdle?" Nana Philly demanded.

But we didn't look back.

"You no-good children, come back here right this instant!" she hollered.

Then we turned the corner and were gone.

A few mornings later, Mrs. Albury turned up at our front door with Little Dizzy on one arm and a basket on the other.

"Helen?" my mother said. "Was something wrong with the laundry?"

"I'm here about Beans."

My mother put her hands on her hips and looked at me. "What did he do?"

Mrs. Albury spoke before I could defend myself. "Your son is a lifesaver!"

"A lifesaver?" my mother repeated.

Mrs. Albury nodded vigorously. "He cured Little Dizzy's diaper rash!"

She pulled a tin out of the basket and passed it to me. I opened it and looked inside. It was full of delicious chocolate divinity.

"I made it for you," she said, and beamed.

"Thanks," I said, blushing.

"No, thank *you*, Beans! You've got a real way with babies!"

Then she kissed me on the cheek and whirled off.

We stood there for a moment.

My mother gave me an amused look. "Real way with babies, huh? Then you can watch Buddy this afternoon."

GOOD HELP

The New Dealers were tearing through town like a hurricane.

Renovation had started on the Casa Marina Hotel. Garbage was being carted away, potholes filled in. Benches were springing up all over town for the mysterious tourists.

Then there were the houses.

Mr. Stone worried there weren't enough places for visitors to sleep. The New Dealers were fixing up falling-apart houses, to be rented out as guesthouses. They were mending roofs. Updating plumbing. Fixing falling-down fences. And they were giving paint to anyone who wanted to give their house a shine.

The colors of the paint were raising eyebrows, though.

The gang and I were standing on Fleming Street, staring at a newly painted house.

It was pink.

"What in the history of cheese?" Pork Chop asked, shaking his head.

"Looks like a baby's bungy," I said.

"There's a blue one over on Elizabeth," Ira said. "Blue as the sky."

"I saw a yellow one on Petronia," Kermit said. "I thought it looked very cheerful."

"You would, Kermit," Pork Chop said.

I shook my head. Pink houses. This place was definitely being run by lunatics.

Johnny Cakes was sitting outside Pepe's Café. He was drinking café con leche. I was pretty sure the can was one of mine. The top edge looked nice and smooth.

"Can we take a walk?" he asked, standing up.

I raised my shoulders. "Sure."

We strolled down Duval.

"So, I'm impressed," he began. "You have an excellent work ethic. Good help is hard to find."

I didn't know what to say, so I just nodded.

He tilted his head. "How would you like to make some real money?"

"What do you mean, real?" The dimes he'd paid us before had seemed pretty real.

"More than a dime," he said.

My eyes widened.

"You see, I find myself in an unexpected situation," he said.

He jerked his head across the street, where a man in Bermuda shorts was striding along with purpose.

"All these do-gooding New Dealers. They're making it very difficult to conduct business in my usual fashion."

"I don't understand," I said.

"I have some valuable *cargo* in my office that needs to go to Miami. My client is anxious. I don't want to disappoint him. Which is where you come in. I'll pay you five dollars."

My head snapped up. Five dollars? I'd be rich!

"What do I have to do?"

He hooked his arm in mine and pulled me into an empty alleyway.

"Ring the fire alarm," he said in a low voice.

"You gonna set something on fire?"

Johnny Cakes frowned. "Don't be ridiculous. I just need a diversion. You set off a fire alarm and the whole town will be focused on the ringing bell. Then I can get my coffins of booze to the boat, and nobody will be the wiser."

"Why don't you just move them in boxes?"

He made a face. "Everyone inspects boxes. Believe me, no one opens coffins."

I could see his point.

"But I can't move all these coffins during the day. It's too suspicious." He looked at me. "So can I count on you?"

I wavered. This seemed different from delivering liquor. *Dirtier* somehow.

But five dollars was a lot of money.

"All right. I'll do it," I told him.

He smiled. "It needs to happen the night after next."

"But what about a fire alarm key?" I asked. "I don't have one."

"You're a smart kid. You'll find one, I'm sure."

He gave me the details and then I turned to leave.

"And, Beans? One more thing."

"Yes?"

He stared at me steadily. "Not a word. To anyone. Understand?"

I nodded.

I was in the outhouse, thinking.

I flipped through the Sears, Roebuck catalog, looking at all the things I would be able to buy with five dollars. The fancy Supertone Deluxe accordion I wanted was twenty-one dollars. Maybe I would have to settle for something less grand, like a harmonica. It was only a dollar and fifteen cents.

Unfortunately, the catalog didn't sell the one thing I desperately needed: a fire alarm key. I had to find one. Problem was, most of my pals lived deep in the lanes, and the fire alarms were on the main streets of Key West.

Except one.

But he wasn't exactly a pal.

Too Bad answered the door on the first knock.

"Beans!" he said excitedly. And then he looked a little confused. "Whatcha doing here?"

I forced myself to say the words. I'd practiced on

the way over. "I've been thinking about letting you into the gang."

Too Bad's face lit up. "You have?"

I held up my bag of marbles. "You need to become a better marble player before the other fellas will accept you. I'm gonna teach you some tricks."

"Gosh. It's my lucky day!"

Or mine.

"We gonna go to your place?" he asked.

I made a face. "The thing is that I don't want to get saddled with watching Buddy, so how about we play here?"

He nodded eagerly. "Sure! You bet! Come on in and I'll get my marbles."

I walked into the house. The fire alarm key was hanging on its hook.

Perfect.

"So, where's your mom today?" I asked in a deliberately bored voice.

"Oh, she's visiting my granny. She won't be back home until supper."

Perfect.

We played marbles all afternoon in his backyard. I let Too Bad beat me three times. Each time he did, it felt like someone was ripping a little bit of my soul out. After the third time, I couldn't take it anymore.

"Say, can I get a glass of water?" I asked him.

"Sure," he said. "Go on inside and help yourself. There's water in the icebox."

Once inside, I ran to the front door, grabbed the key, and pocketed it quick. Then I walked back to the kitchen. There was water in a pitcher in the icebox, so I filled two glasses and brought them outside.

When Too Bad's mother came home, she gave us each a big slice of cake.

"Look at you boys playing so nicely back here!" She smiled.

"Beans is teaching me some tricks, Mama!" Too Bad told her.

I almost felt guilty for stealing the key.

ACADEMY AWARD

Shirley Temple had better watch out. Because I could act.

It was almost nine o'clock when I yawned dramatically.

"I think I'll go up to bed now," I told my mother.

"A bit early for you, isn't it?"

"Just tired, I guess. Good night."

I lay in bed, listening to her putter around in her bedroom. Finally, everything was quiet. Even Buddy was asleep. I went downstairs and slipped out the back door, pretending I was going to the outhouse, in case she woke up. But there was no noise from her room, and I knew I was home free. I slipped off my pajamas and put on pants and a shirt. Then I started walking fast.

When I reached Frances Street, I heard something behind me. I whirled around and there was Termite.

"What are you doing following me?" I asked in exasperation.

The dog sat on his haunches and wagged his tail at me, drooling.

"Go home!" I ordered, pointing to Curry Lane.

He cocked his head at me as if confused.

"Go!" I said in a low voice, and he finally got up and waddled back the way he'd come.

Johnny Cakes was waiting for me behind his building. Three wagons with horses and drivers were lined up.

"You remember the plan?" he asked me.

"Yes," I said. "Pull the alarm on White and Catherine."

He put his hand on my shoulder. "Good boy. Don't let me down."

I walked quickly through the dark, quiet streets. When I reached the fire alarm, I looked around nervously. I heard a noise and ducked behind a ragged bush.

A moment later, our resident writer and another fella stumbled by, singing loudly about dames.

When the coast was clear, I moved quickly before I could lose my nerve. I fumbled with the key and struggled to open the alarm. Then I triggered it.

The ringing bell sang through the quiet night.

I took off running. By the time I slipped into my backyard, the sound of the fire engine had joined the chorus. I quickly put on my pajamas, took a deep breath, and slammed the outhouse door as loud as I could.

When I walked into the kitchen, my mother and Kermit were looking at the fire alarm card.

"Beans! Beans! Fire bell went off!" Kermit declared.

"I heard when I was out there doing my business," I said, feigning surprise. "Where's it at?"

"White and Catherine!" Kermit said.

"How about that," I said, and yawned. "Well, I'm gonna go back to bed."

The ringing sang me to sleep.

• • •

The next morning, I dropped by Too Bad's and we played a game of marbles. I slipped the fire key onto the hook on my way out, with no one the wiser.

Then I went to see Johnny Cakes. His office was completely empty. There wasn't a coffin in sight.

"Next time, you will pull more alarms," he said firmly. "I was nearly caught."

"Sorry," I said.

"Still, you did good, kid. I just might have to put you on my payroll permanently." He handed me a roll of bills and winked, adding, "By the way, I gave you a little bonus."

I counted out the money. He had given me an extra five dollars. I had never held so much money in my whole life.

I felt like Daddy Warbucks.

Except with hair.

This time when I walked into Gardner's Pharmacy, the ringing bell on the door sounded like a choir of angels singing "Hallelujah." My eyes took in every shelf, all the glittering bottles and big jars of candy.

"Why, hello, Beans," Mr. Gardner said. "Do you need more Bumstead's for Kermit?"

"Not today," I said with satisfaction. "I'm looking for the best ladies' hand cream you got."

"Ladies' hand cream, you say?"

"For my mother."

There was a shelf with a mirror over it filled with cosmetics. Mr. Gardner pulled down a small jar. It had a fancy label that said PACQUIN'S HAND CREAM.

"This one's very good," he said. He raised a questioning eyebrow. "But it's five dollars."

"That's fine," I said, and handed him the money.

"You're a sweet boy," Mr. Gardner said.

My mother's reaction wasn't quite as pleased.

"Where did you get the money for this?" she demanded suspiciously.

I lied like a grown-up. "Just been picking up a whole lot of cans."

"And you spent it on this?"

I nodded.

Her face softened. "Thank you, son."

Honestly, I deserved an Academy Award.

PARTY LINE

The front porch was the coolest place to be during the heat of the day. The ceiling was painted a watery blue-green that looked like the sky. Most of the porch ceilings in Key West were this color. Conchs called it haint blue, and it was supposed to keep haints away. If I was a ghost, I wouldn't haunt these shabby little houses. I'd haunt somewhere nice, like a mansion. But maybe ghosts were just like the living and were down on their luck.

Kermit moaned from where he sat on the step.

"What's wrong with you?" I asked him.

"My throat hurts."

Pork Chop came running down the block.

"Beans! Your pa's on the horn!" he hollered.

"Stay here," I told Kermit, and took off running.

Mrs. Soldano handed me the phone when I walked in the door.

"Poppy!" I said. "Where are you?"

His voice sounded watery and far away.

"I'm in New Jersey. At your aunt's house."

The line was choppy. I could hear someone listening. Judging by the giggles, it was probably that Dot. She had a phone at her house.

"Can you tell your mother that nothing's changed?"

I knew what that meant: he still didn't have a job.

"Okay," I said.

"And tell her that I love her, and give your brothers a hug for me."

"I will," I promised.

"Don't forget: you're the man of the house."

How could I?

After he hung up, I stayed on the line. Someone laughed again.

"I know it's you, Dot!" I shouted.

"Man of the house? You're not man enough to play me in marbles."

Then she hung up. I hated that girl.

When I told Ma about the phone call with Poppy, her whole body went still.

"Ma?" I said. "Are you okay?"

She straightened her shoulders and smiled.

"I'm fine."

"Are *we* gonna be okay?"

"Of course," she said, but the smile didn't reach her eyes. "Everything's just fine."

That's when I realized that sometimes adults lied because it was easier than telling the truth.

A few days later, when my mother walked in the door, her smile was genuine.

"Mrs. Higgs wants me to make a custom dress for her!" she said. "Isn't that thrilling?"

That didn't sound thrilling.

"She's going to pay me nine dollars!"

Now it sounded downright exciting.

"But I'm gonna need a sewing machine. I can get

one secondhand down on Duval for twenty-five dollars," she said, and looked at me. "I need your help."

"My help?" I squeaked.

I felt a wave of panic. Did she know about me working for Johnny Cakes? Even I didn't get paid that much.

Ma put her hands on my shoulders and looked me in the eyes. "I need you to go ask Nana Philly for the money. I promise to pay her back."

I was confused. "You want *me* to ask *her*?"

She sighed. "If I go, she'll just complain about your father and how I made my own bed and I should lie in it. It's much better if you do it. She'd have to be harder than the devil himself to say no to a child."

I wanted to tell her the devil was probably scared of Nana Philly.

"Just think. If this works out, I can take in less laundry," Ma said. "And it'll be easier on my hands."

I gave in. "Okay," I agreed. "I'll do it."

"You're a good boy," she said with a smile. Then she plucked something black off the kitchen counter.

It was Nana Philly's girdle.

"I found this under the mattress in Buddy's crib. I don't know how it got there," she said, shaking her head.

"It's a mystery," I said.

• • •

As Kermit and I walked over, I looked at the girdle.

"I'm gonna miss this," I said. "It's the only thing that kept Buddy in that crib."

Kermit shook his head and swallowed, wincing. He looked a little pale. "This ain't gonna work."

"Let me do the talking," I told him.

When we reached the house, I knocked on the door. No one answered.

Kermit grinned.

"Huh, would you look at that? She's not home. Guess we'll have to go!"

Before his foot hit the bottom step, the door banged open.

"What do you want?"

"Ma found your girdle," I said, holding it out.

She snatched it from my hand. She started to shut the door when I wedged my foot inside.

"Can we come in for a minute? Kermit's real thirsty."

She looked suspiciously at Kermit. "Humph. Come on, then. What are you waiting for?"

If any place in Key West was haunted, it was Nana Philly's house. Everything in it was old. There were oil paintings and an ancient piano and expensive china

83

cups. Thick old rugs and heavy velvet curtains. My great-grandfather had been a wrecker. He'd salvaged boats that crashed in the treacherous Keys, and claimed the cargo—silver, furniture, silk, you name it.

"I hear that your father still doesn't have a job," she said bluntly.

Of course she'd heard. I'm sure the whole town knew. Conchs liked to gossip. Ma joked that you couldn't keep anything secret because of the "Conch Telegraph."

She shook her head. "I told your mother not to marry a Curry, but did she believe me?"

I didn't say anything. I knew better.

"Nobody's going to hire him up north. I've been there."

"You have?" This was news to me. "When?"

"When I was a girl. I didn't like it one little bit. People are different there. They'll never hire your father. Mark my words." Her eyes narrowed and she got straight to the point. "So why are you really here?"

I shook my head. A tiny part of me admired her: she would never get Winkied.

"So, Nana Philly," I said. "This lady wants Ma to make her a dress. Ain't that swell?"

She grunted.

"The thing is, Ma needs money for a sewing machine."

She pursed her lips. "So she sent you over here to ask for the money?"

I nodded.

"How much does she need?" she asked.

I told her.

"That's ridiculous!" she shouted.

Kermit looked like he was going to faint from fear.

Nana Philly studied me sharply. "What do you think about this idea of hers?"

"Me?" Since when did grown-ups ask kids what they thought?

"Yes, *you*."

"Well, she's good at sewing," I said, and pointed to a patch on my pants.

"I taught her how to sew," Nana Philly told me. She sounded wistful. For a moment, she seemed like a different person.

Almost . . . *nice?*

"Really?" I asked her.

"But she was always terrible at hems!" she snapped.

Just like that, the mean old lady was back.

• • •

Nana Philly didn't give me the money, which wasn't much of a surprise. A hobo could crawl up her steps and faint from hunger and she wouldn't give him a dime.

To make matters worse, she insisted that Kermit swallow a concoction she whipped up for his throat.

"Drink it," she ordered him.

"It smells funny," my brother said, sniffing the cup suspiciously.

She just grabbed the cup, pinched his nose, and poured it down his throat. He coughed and his ears turned red. Then he let out a wail and ran from the house, screeching.

I turned to her.

"What was in it?" I asked.

She looked at me. "Horseradish, of course. Best thing for a sore throat."

My mother shook her head when I told her what had happened.

"I don't know what I was expecting," she muttered to herself. "I guess I'll have to hand-stitch the dress."

That night as we lay in bed, Kermit couldn't stop talking about Nana Philly.

"She tried to kill me, Beans! My own grandmother tried to kill me!" he said.

"Well, you're still alive, so she did a bad job of it," I observed.

"It's only 'cause I ran away. She would've finished me off for sure! You'd be really sad if I was dead."

"I'd have the room to myself, at least," I pointed out.

But I was kind of curious.

"How's your throat feel?" I asked my brother.

Kermit yawned and rolled over. "Better."

I lay in bed wondering if Nana Philly was right about Poppy not getting work.

What if the meanest grown-up in Key West was also the only one telling the truth?

DUELING WITH DOT

In the pictures, it seemed so easy to settle fights: just have a duel. Two swords, some fancy footwork, and a clear winner. In real life, it wasn't as simple. Especially when girls were involved.

My duel with Dot started over pineapple.

There was a factory on Eaton that canned pineapple from Cuba. Shipments of pineapple arrived at odd times, and they were always cause for celebration for us kids. Because when the workers processed the pineapple, they discarded the cores in a huge pile behind the factory. There's nothing sweeter than a fresh pine-apple core on a hot day.

I was sitting on our front porch when Pork Chop rode up on his bike.

"You hear the news?" he asked me.

"Hear what?"

"Mami is really angry!" Pork Chop exclaimed. "The Kingfish wants to ban bolita!"

That's what folks were calling Mr. Stone—the Kingfish of Key West—'cause he was so bossy.

"Why would he ban bolita?"

My best pal made a face. "Says gambling ain't good for getting tourists."

That didn't make any sense. Everybody loved to gamble, as far as I could tell. Key West's best busi-nesses were gambling and liquor.

"Did you go by Eaton Street this morning?" I asked him.

"Pineapple ain't in yet," he said. Then he patted his back pocket. "I gotta go deliver these bolita numbers for Mami now. She don't want Mr. Stone showing up in our kitchen."

I was still sitting on the porch when lunchtime

rolled around. A couple of kids were whizzing down Frances on bikes. Dot was one of the kids. She slowed as she passed me.

"Where's everybody going? Pineapple?" I said.

"Big marble tournament," she said. "Why? You wanna play me?"

"'Course not," I said. "Keepsies don't play girls."

"Have it your way," she said, and pedaled off.

The next morning, Kermit and me went to Pork Chop's house. The gang was already there.

"Any word on the pineapple?" I asked Pork Chop.

He looked confused. "What're you talking about?"

"When's it coming in?"

"It came in. Right around noon yesterday."

"What?" I demanded.

"I figured you'd heard. Every single kid in town was there."

Realization dawned on me.

"She tricked me," I said slowly.

"Who tricked you?" Ira asked.

"Dot! I saw her go by on her bicycle, and she swore the pineapple hadn't come in!"

Pork Chop gave me a look. "And you believed her?"

I shook my head in dismay.

Dot had Winkied me.

Ma came home carrying two cans and a couple of brushes.

"What's that, Ma?" I asked.

"Paint from the New Dealers," she replied.

I lifted a lid. The paint was pink.

"Really, Ma?" I asked.

"Beggars can't be choosers. I wanted green, but it had all been taken."

She went inside, but I sat there on the front porch staring at the pink paint.

Then I slowly grinned.

"You gotta see it!" Pork Chop exclaimed, Ira hot on his heels.

"See what?" I asked.

"Just come!" Ira said.

Pork Chop smirked. "It's the most hilarious thing you've ever seen, brother!"

We went behind a house on Love Lane and peered into the backyard.

"Look!" Pork Chop said.

Painted on the old outhouse was:

Queen Dot's Throne

In pink paint.

There was even a pink crown.

Pork Chop chortled. "Isn't that a riot, pal?"

"It's a regular work of art!" Ira said.

I had to agree: the artist had talent.

Queen Dot's Throne started showing up on outhouses all around town. Nobody knew who was doing it. Rumor was that the mysterious painter struck in the dark of night, like the mysterious Shadow on the radio show.

Me and the gang were playing marbles in front of my house when Dot came storming up. She was spitting like a cat.

"I know it's you!" she shouted.

"I don't know what you're talking about," I said, all innocence.

"You're the one who's painting 'Queen Dot's Throne' on outhouses!"

I looked at the fellas as if shocked. "It ain't me. It's probably one of them New Dealer artists."

"It is *so* you! Freckles over on Pinder Lane saw you slipping out of a backyard with a paintbrush."

I held out my hands. "You see paint on these hands? Must've been someone else. I've just got a familiar face."

She shook with rage and then whirled around and marched away.

We burst out laughing.

A few days later, the gang and I were knee-deep in dirt, playing a game of marbles, when a barefoot girl with pigtails came running up to me.

"Beans Curry!" she said. "Your mama's been hollering for you for the last half hour."

"I didn't hear her," I said.

It was the truth.

The girl put her hands on her hips and cocked her head. "Well, she said you better get your bungy down to the kraals and pick up some turtle meat on credit, or you ain't gonna have no supper."

Then she turned and ran off.

I stood up. "Guess I better go, fellas."

"Can I stay here? I don't wanna do chores," Kermit whined.

"Fine, stay. I'll pick you up after."

I ran down to the kraals as fast as my legs could carry me. When Ma hollered, you ran.

There was a little shack at the edge where you could put in your order. An older man stood behind a wooden counter.

"Hi, Mr. Thompson," I said. "Ma sent me to get some meat on credit."

"Sure thing, Beans. Give me a few minutes to butcher some meat for you."

"I'll wait outside," I told him. I kind of liked the turtles; I didn't really want to see one chopped up.

I sat near the turtle kraals, peering down into the water. The big creatures were swimming lazily, their shells appearing, then disappearing beneath the dark surface.

I felt someone push me. Before I could see who it was, I found myself flying through the air. I landed in the water and sank. When I came up, I was gasping for air, and turtles were bumping into me on every side. Now I knew how it felt to be tossed into the kraals.

Terrible.

I heard laughter and looked up. Dot was grinning down at me.

"You look like a turned turtle!" she hooted.

Standing next to her was . . . *the girl with the pigtails?*

"You!" I spit out. "Did my mother even call for me?"

She pretended to think hard for a moment, and then she looked at Dot. "Boys sure are easy to fool."

"You said it," Dot agreed.

I hated that girl.

Come to think of it, I hated both of them.

DOG DAYS

Avery had his easel set up, and he was working on another picture of a little Conch house. It was one that the New Dealers had recently given a pink paint job. This time, his picture matched real life.

"You sure like painting houses," I told him.

Avery dabbed watery blue under the roof eaves of the house.

"Why don't you paint something exciting?" I asked him.

"What do you suggest?"

I threw up my hands. "I don't know. How about a sword fight?"

He chuckled. "A sword fight? Does this look like a Hollywood set?"

"I bet that the whole world would want to visit Key West if there were sword fights."

His mouth twitched in amusement. "You might be onto something."

I sat there and watched him paint for a while.

"What's it like in Hollywood?" I asked.

"It's like anywhere else," he said with a shrug.

"But it must be exciting!"

"Hollywood isn't very exciting, kid. It's hard work and long hours. It's like anything else: a job."

I stared at his painting. "Do you really think Mr. Stone sending out postcards and brochures will make people come here?"

"I don't see why not. It's all about telling a good story. Just like a Hollywood picture."

"What's the story?"

He waved his paintbrush. "'Come discover a hidden gem, Key West. Where the weather is balmy, the ocean breeze sweet, and the architecture unique.' You would have a starring role as the Charming Local Boy."

"That sounds like a pretty boring picture to me," I told him.

He rolled his eyes.

Then I smiled. "Say, could you get me a screen test with Warner Brothers?"

I wasn't the only one wondering about what Mr. Stone was doing. Lots of folks were talking. And not all the talk was good.

"I hear they're going after the dogs!" Kermit said.

"The dogs?" Pork Chop said in disbelief. "Tell it to Sweeney!"

"It's true!" Kermit insisted. "Mr. Stone says they're a nuisance."

Now that I thought about it, I hadn't seen quite as many strays around the lanes lately.

We saw the dogcatchers in action the next day. We were playing marbles in the cemetery—there were always good patches of dirt to be found there. A bunch of New Dealers had cornered a dog on Frances Street. One fella had a fisherman's net, and the other had a small chunk of meat. He tossed the meat to the dog, who lunged. As soon as the dog started eating, the other fella threw the net over the hound and dragged it off, yipping.

"What are you going to do about your dog?" Ira asked.

The hound in question was fast asleep on a gravestone.

I didn't know when Termite had become my dog, but he had. Or maybe I'd become his person.

Either way, I needed to keep him safe.

I tried out some more of my acting on Ma that night. I explained what was going on with the dogcatchers and asked if I could keep Termite in the house.

"Inside?" she asked dubiously.

"I'm just so lonely with Poppy gone," I told her dramatically. "Please?"

She sighed heavily.

"I suppose so," she said, shaking her head. "What's one more pest in this house?"

But bolita and dogs were just the beginning.

Mr. Stone came after us kids next.

We were on Fleming Street with a big pack of kids, playing marbles, when Mr. Stone came storming up in his Bermuda shorts.

I was just getting ready to shoot when he demanded, "What are you doing, Peas?"

"Beans," I said.

"Of course," he said. "Now, can you please answer my question: what are you doing?"

All the kids turned to me like I was the Big Cheese.

"We're playing marbles. I'm beating Too Bad here," I said.

Too Bad nodded. "He sure is! Second time this morning!"

Mr. Stone wagged his finger at us. "You children need to get out of the street."

"Why?" I asked.

"Because it's *dangerous*!"

"It's dangerous playing marbles?"

"You could get hit by a car!" he said.

What cars?

"Luckily, I have an excellent solution," he declared. "Follow me!"

Like the Pied Piper, he led us down streets and lanes, halfway across town.

"Here we are," he announced, stopping in front of a vacant lot.

The ground was swampy, with buzzing mosquitoes

everywhere. There was a simple wooden seesaw in the middle of the lot, and a dried-out coconut palm listed in the back.

"Isn't this lovely?" he enthused. "Look, there's a seesaw! Isn't that nice?"

"Uh, I guess," I said.

He clasped his hands. "It will make a much better impression if tourists don't see a bunch of children running wild in the street."

"So this is like a jail?"

"No, of course not!" Mr. Stone said with a wave. "This is called a playground."

"A playground?" I repeated.

He said with exaggerated slowness, "It. Is. Where. Children. Play."

I blinked at him.

He clapped his hands. "Have. Fun. Playing!"

Then he walked away.

I realized Avery was right. Mr. Stone was making a Hollywood movie called *Key West*. And he didn't want any kids acting in the movie.

We'd just been left on the cutting-room floor.

LESSONS

It was September, and all across Key West, kids were bawling their eyes out. Because even though almost everyone had been laid off, the town still somehow managed to employ the teachers. Which meant we had to go back to school.

The grammar school was on Division Street, and my mother liked to tell us we were "going to Division Street to learn division."

Hardy-har.

On our way to school, we saw men working. Mr.

Stone directed them as they carried a tall metal can of some kind.

"On the corner, please," he instructed them, and they put it down with a bang.

He saw me standing there. "What do you think, Peas?"

"It's Beans."

"Of course," he said. "So what do you think of the trash receptacles?"

"Huh?"

"The garbage cans," he explained. "We bought them at considerable expense. I think it will make a real difference."

He was spending money to put garbage cans around Key West? What was he gonna do next? Put gold and diamonds on outhouses?

I just shook my head.

In my opinion, it was the grown-ups who needed to go back to school.

There was a big map of the world on the wall in our schoolroom. I found myself staring at New Jersey, wondering about Poppy. It seemed very far away.

Our teacher's name was Miss Sugarapple, but there

was nothing sweet about her. She liked to give us tests. Seemed like we were having one every day.

Today it was a geography quiz.

"You have a half hour to complete this test," Miss Sugarapple told us.

Around the room, pencils started flying. But I just stared at my paper. We were supposed to write the names of countries in Europe, and I didn't even know where to begin. If she'd given us a test on the names of the lanes of Key West, I'd get an A.

There was a knock at the classroom door, and a little boy appeared.

"Principal wants to see you, Miss Sugarapple," the kid said, and our teacher followed him out.

The minute the door shut, I stood up. I might not be good at geography, but I knew where things were located.

I walked up to Miss Sugarapple's desk and borrowed a pencil to make it appear that I wasn't doing anything wrong. My eyes scanned the desk, looking for the answer sheet.

"Hurry!" Pork Chop said.

Every kid in the room had stopped what they were doing to watch me.

Finally, I found the answer sheet under a grocery list. I had started to stuff it down my pants when our teacher walked in and her eyes met mine.

My punishment was to stay after school and write *I will not steal* two hundred times on the chalkboard. In cursive.

"I hope you've learned your lesson," Miss Sugarapple told me.

I had. The next time, I would just stick the answer sheet up my shirt.

I wasn't the only one getting into trouble at school, though.

We were doing our spelling lesson when I heard barking. Very *familiar* barking.

A while later, I was called into the principal's office. Mr. Mahon was a cranky-looking man with a bushy mustache. I didn't blame him for being cranky. I wouldn't want to work here, either.

"Follow me," he said.

Waiting outside the front door, barking his head off, was Termite.

"I understand this is your dog," Mr. Mahon said. "He's been barking outside all morning."

"Sorry," I said. "He must have got out and followed me here."

I walked Termite home and put him in the house. He was back barking at the school by lunchtime.

Termite was an even worse student than me.

Some kids would do anything to avoid going to school. They'd say they had a bellyache or their ears hurt. Kermit was fond of this trick. The kid said he felt sick nearly every other day.

The sun was up and I was already dressed and ready to go, but Kermit refused to get out of bed.

"Shake a leg," I told him. "Or we're gonna be tardy."

The lump of blankets didn't move. I knew he was just pretending to be asleep.

Termite whined.

"Maybe he's dead and we'll finally have the room to ourselves," I said to my dog as I walked over to my brother.

I yanked the blanket off Kermit.

"Get up—" I started to say, and then gasped.

He was soaking wet.

"Did you have an accident?" I asked, shaking him.

Kermit blinked up at me in confusion.

"My throat hurts," he croaked.

Kermit burned with fever. He cried, saying his throat hurt and his ankles, too. He lay in bed, drifting in and out of sleep. That's when I knew he was really sick. No kid wants to stay in bed *all* day, even to avoid school.

My mother fetched the doctor.

"Your boy's got rheumatic fever," he told her.

My mother paled. "What do I do?"

"Give him aspirin to keep his fever down. But other than that, he just needs to stay in bed and rest."

"But he'll be fine, won't he?" my mother asked.

"I'm not going to sugarcoat it. If his heart is stressed, he could die," the doctor said.

"Die?" I whispered.

"Yes," he replied.

I looked in the bedroom at my brother shivering in the bed. For the first time in my life, I wished a grown-up would lie to me.

ARITHMETIC

I ended up getting my own room after all.

Not because Kermit died, but because he got better.

"Your son must stay in bed. There should be no physical exertion at all," the doctor told my mother. "It could damage his heart."

"For how long?" my mother asked.

"Six months at least," he told her.

My mouth dropped open. My mother's mouth dropped open. We could have caught a swarm of mosquitoes between us.

It turned out I could handle bad babies but I couldn't

handle Kermit. He whined for water. He whined for me to tuck in his blanket. He whined for me to bring him some toast. Could I read him a book? And on and on and on.

Even Termite kept his distance from Kermit. I think my little brother was driving my dog nuts, too. That's when my mother decided to give Kermit Buddy's bedroom. We moved the crib into my parents' room.

Not to mention I changed my mind about what I would buy from the Sears, Roebuck catalog if I was rich. Forget accordions: I wanted a toilet!

See, Kermit wasn't allowed to go downstairs to use the outhouse because it might strain his heart. So my mother put a pot in the corner of his bedroom for him to do his business. Guess whose job it was to empty the pot? Me.

Everyone at school felt sorry for Kermit.

Miss Sugarapple paused by my desk one day.

"How is your poor brother doing, Beans?" my teacher asked me, her voice dripping with sympathy.

I shrugged.

Her voice lowered. "Is he going to live?"

"Unfortunately," I said.

• • •

Kermit was bored from being in bed all day, so the minute I got home from school, he started hollering for me.

"Beans! Beans! Come upstairs!"

"Go on and keep him company," my mother said.

"Do I have to?" I begged.

She just looked at me. "He's your brother. He almost died. You should be happy to spend time with him."

I groaned.

"Besides, I have to run some errands. I'll take Buddy with me. I'll be back in a little bit."

But I knew my mother was lying. She was sick of Kermit, too.

When I got to Kermit's room, he was sitting up in his bed. He'd lost some weight and still looked a little pale, but his mouth worked just fine.

"What'd you do in school today, Beans? How're the fellas? Did you see that it rained right after lunchtime? Want to play cards?"

The questions poured from Kermit's mouth in a rush. It almost made me wish I was back in school. Which was saying something, considering the day I'd had.

Miss Sugarapple had handed back our arithmetic tests. I got a bad mark on mine. I don't even want to say how bad.

"If you practice more, you'll get better," she told me.

I'd been practicing arithmetic since I'd first stepped into the school, and I never got better at it. Besides, I wasn't the only one who was bad at arithmetic. President Roosevelt wasn't much of a whiz, seeing how the country was still in a depression.

Termite started barking like mad, and I looked out the window, worried that dogcatchers were coming.

But it was just the postman.

"Call off your hound, Beans!" he hollered. "I got a letter for your ma."

"Termite!" I shouted. "Quit it!"

The dog crawled under the porch.

"That dog of yours is a menace," the postman grumbled as he handed me a letter.

"He's all bark, honest," I told him.

But he just frowned and walked away.

I looked at the letter and recognized the slanted handwriting; it was from Poppy.

I opened it and read quickly.

Dear Minnie,

How is Kermit doing? I know you said the worst had passed and I shouldn't rush back home, but I feel terrible. If things change, I can always borrow money from my sister to get back.

I met with the man at the factory again, but he said he had to wait and see about hiring.

I wish I had better news, but I don't.

Hope all is well in Conch Town. I miss you and the boys more than you can know.

Love,
Your Curry husband

I might not have been good at arithmetic, but I knew that Poppy not getting work plus his not coming home would equal my mother being upset.

Better for her to wait and read good news rather than this bad news.

I went to the outhouse and did my duty. Instead of the Sears, Roebuck catalog, I used the letter. Paper was paper.

It was all scratchy on your bungy.

SHOES

Girls were confusing. They got excited about things that boys didn't. Even my mother.

She was standing in front of me, holding the dress she'd made.

"I finished it, Beans," she announced. "What do you think?"

I thought it looked like a lady's dress with some green ribbon, but I wasn't going to tell her that.

"Sure looks nice," I told her.

She wrapped it up carefully and put it in a basket.

"I'm going to deliver this to Mrs. Higgs now," she

told me. "Feed your brothers breakfast. I'll stop at the store on the way home so we can have an extra-nice treat for supper tonight."

She practically bounded outside.

We'd barely finished breakfast when Ma walked back in the front door.

"What'd you get for supper, Ma?" I asked her.

"Nothing," she said, sounding defeated. "Mrs. Higgs didn't pay me."

"She didn't pay you?"

"She said the dress wasn't up to her standards. That she expected machine stitching. She said she 'won't pay for bad work,'" my mother recited, and pulled the dress out of the basket and stared at it.

Then she sat down at the table and put her face in her hands.

"All that time. For nothing," she whispered, and she sounded like her heart was broken. "I can't believe it."

But I wasn't surprised about it one bit.

It was just like a grown-up to lie.

At school, I couldn't concentrate. Everything just flew by me: the teacher's words, the numbers on the page, the letters in my reader. I had known that things were bad, but my mother's tears had let loose something in me: fear.

So when Johnny Cakes asked me to set off the fire alarm bell again, I said yes. I felt a twinge of guilt when I thought of Cem and the other firefighters. But then I pictured my father up north in New Jersey begging for work, and the devastated look on my mother's face, and I hardened my heart. Someone had to do something.

Like Poppy said: I was the man of the house now.

I looked Johnny Cakes square in the eye. "I want more money this time."

Me and Johnny Cakes met in his office to make the plan. He had a map of Key West spread out on his desk. There were little Xs by all the fire alarm boxes around town.

"I don't want to get caught, like I nearly was before," he said, tapping the map. "You need to buy me more time."

"So what should I do?"

He stared at the map. "Set off alarms as far away from each other as possible. I have a lot to load up. And make sure none are near the route my truck will be going."

I looked across the room at the pile of coffins.

In the end, we picked four alarm boxes around town.

"I don't want to leave anything to chance," Johnny Cakes told me. "You need to do a practice run."

That's how I found myself racing through the streets of Key West, trying out the route. I skirted the alarm boxes so as not to draw attention. When I made it back to Johnny Cakes's place, he looked pleased.

"That should give me plenty of time," he said.

"Good," I said, panting.

Then he looked down at my dirty bare feet.

"Don't you have any shoes?"

"No," I said. "I can run just fine without them."

"What if you step on something? A piece of glass? I'm buying you a pair."

He was like a mother hen. The criminal version.

After Johnny Cakes bought me new shoes, I stopped by Too Bad's to play marbles. I let him win twice and left with the fire alarm key in my back pocket.

Maybe we should start calling him Too Easy.

The following night, I waited in bed until the house was quiet. Then I slipped out the back door, holding my new shoes.

Problem was, I didn't have socks. Hadn't even thought about it when Johnny Cakes bought me the shoes. But there wasn't much I could do about it now, so I just put the shoes on anyway.

I started running.

Pulling the alarms felt a little easier this time. Maybe because more was at stake than going to the pictures or buying ice cream. This Depression was bearing down on my family like a hurricane. One good wind would sweep us away. I needed to blow us in the other direction.

The first two alarms went off fine. Things got sticky when I arrived at the third one. Literally. Some stupid kid had put gum in the keyhole, and I couldn't get the key in.

I gave up and headed to the last alarm, the sound of the fire engine clanging in the background. My feet were killing me. The new shoes rubbed against my bare heels. By the time I reached Too Bad's house, it felt like someone was shoving a knife into them. I couldn't take it anymore. So I took off the shoes and threw them in the first garbage can I passed.

All I had left to do was to return the key.

• • •

Everyone seemed to be asleep at Too Bad's house; I could hear his father snoring through an open window upstairs. It was almost louder than the fire bell. I quietly opened the front door and slipped the key back in its place.

I limped home on my bare feet.

CHASING HAINTS

Every kid in school was buzzing about what had happened the night before.

"Did you hear all the fire bells ringing last night?" Pork Chop asked me.

"I didn't hear a thing," I said. "Slept like a baby!"

Which was a dumb thing to say because, in my experience, babies were lousy sleepers.

"Kids are saying it was a prank," Ira said.

"Hey, fellas! Whatcha talking about?" a voice asked behind me.

I looked back. Too Bad was standing there. And he was wearing ... *my shoes?*

"Where'd you get those shoes?" I asked him.

He gave a happy smile. "Found 'em in a garbage can. They're practically brand-new!"

"They look real comfortable," I said.

After school, I walked past the firehouse on my way to Johnny Cakes's place.

Cem was sitting out front, clutching a cup of leche like his life depended on it. There were dark bags under his eyes, and he was practically falling asleep where he sat.

"Cem," I said. "You okay?"

He blinked and shook his head. "I was up all night chasing haints."

"What?"

"All the fire alarms were false. Weren't any real fires."

I looked at him awkwardly. "Sorry to hear that."

Johnny Cakes, on the other hand, was grinning from ear to ear.

"Good job, kid. Nobody suspected a thing," he said when I got to his office. "But we'll probably have to come up with some other scheme for next time."

"Next time?" I asked as he counted out the money into my hand.

Johnny Cakes raised an eyebrow. "Don't you like working for me?"

Did I? Maybe the first few times I had. But now it tasted like milk after the ice in the icebox had melted: spoiled. Not that I could tell Johnny Cakes.

"I like it just fine," I lied.

My mother was doing laundry in the backyard when I got home.

"Here ya go, Ma," I said, and handed her nine dollars from my Johnny Cakes earnings. I'd kept a dollar for myself. I figured I'd earned it.

Or at least my feet had.

"What's this?" she asked.

"Mrs. Higgs paid up for the dress."

She sounded shocked. "What?"

"I went by her house and told her it wasn't fair, what she did. She gave me the money."

"I can't believe it," she said, shaking her head.

"But if I was you, I wouldn't work for her again."

"I wouldn't lift a hand for that woman if she fainted in front of me. Thank you, son," she said, and smiled.

Then she looked down at my feet.

"Good heavens. What happened to your feet?"

The lie tripped off my tongue. "I just took a tumble."

"My poor, sweet boy," she said.

She bandaged them up.

There was a new Shirley Temple picture playing, so I treated myself to the late show. I even got popcorn. I thought about sitting in the balcony, but decided against it because of the situation with the haint last time.

The picture was hilarious. Shirley Temple just got better and better. I found myself studying her, trying to pick up her tricks. She had a good smile, and she knew how to use it. I wondered if maybe I should start smiling more.

Nah.

When the credits started rolling, I stood, glancing up at the balcony.

I gasped.

The man with the gloves was sitting there. He was holding the cane.

Then he got up and disappeared.

I couldn't help myself. I ran through the theater and followed him as he slipped out the back door and into a little alley. He was gone again. A moment later, I caught a glimpse of him as he reappeared from the inky shadows far ahead.

I trailed him through the dark streets. He moved pretty fast for a haint, although he favored one leg and used the cane. As we neared the cemetery, he slowed down. He stopped suddenly at Poor House Lane. Then he straightened his shoulders and turned around.

I gasped in horror when I saw his nose. In the light of the moon, it looked like it was melting off!

"Why are you following me?" he demanded in a low voice.

"You're alive!"

He made a small sound. "Do I look like I'm dead?"

"Bring Back My Hammer said you were a haint!"

He barked a laugh. "I suppose you could say I am, in a manner of speaking."

"I don't understand."

The man looked at me. "Who are your people?"

"I'm a Curry."

"I knew a girl who married a Curry boy. She was very beautiful. We were in school together. Her name was Minerva. Do you know her?"

"She's my mother," I said.

He tilted his head. "Is she still lovely?"

I nodded. This was the strangest conversation I'd ever had in my entire life.

"Why did Bring Back My Hammer lie and say you were a haint?" I asked the man.

He gave a heavy sigh and then said, "Do you know what leprosy is?"

"Like the lepers in the Bible?"

"Yes. I have leprosy. That's why I go to the late show. I can't come out during the day."

"Why not?"

"It's not safe. Especially with all these strangers in town. They'd send me to the leper hospital in Louisiana. Nobody ever comes back from that place."

"Oh," I said.

"I'm not the only one," he said. "There's a few of us in the lanes. Our families keep us hidden. Nobody really pays attention if we go out at night. Bring Back My Hammer is my cousin, so he lets me into the late shows."

I didn't know what to say after that. It seemed so . . . *sad.*

"So, uh, you like the pictures?" I asked.

"Yes!" he said, sounding excited. "I see everything that comes to the theater!"

"Say, have you seen Baby LeRoy?"

"Who hasn't? Did you know that he got a diaper endorsement?"

"Really?"

He nodded. "My sister-in-law gets me the Hollywood magazines. I just read about it."

"That baby's gonna be big!"

We stood in the shadows on Poor House Lane and talked about the pictures.

It wasn't until I was home in bed that I realized I hadn't asked him his name.

SMOKE

Ma was back to taking in laundry, which meant I was back to delivering it.

As I pulled the wagon with clean clothes down the little lanes, I found myself studying houses with new eyes. Which ones hid lepers?

But something more surprising than a leper was waiting for me when I reached Nana Philly's house: Avery.

He had his easel set up, and he was painting a picture of her house.

"Well, look who it is," he said to me.

He was dabbing some yellow paint onto his brush. I wanted to tell him he should be using red because this was where the devil lived.

"Don't you know who lives here?"

"I'm afraid not."

"This is Nana Philly's house."

"I see."

I gave him a look. "She hasn't come out and, um, *hollered* at you yet?"

He looked up from his painting. "Why would she do that?"

"Because she doesn't like people."

"Maybe she has a soft spot for artists."

"Mr. Avery, Nana Philly ain't got a soft spot for anybody. Believe me, I would know."

He raised an eyebrow.

"I'm her grandson," I explained.

Well, there was no putting it off. I took her pile of clean laundry and walked up the porch steps.

"Nana Philly," I called. "Got your laundry."

But nobody answered. Was she out?

I walked across the porch and peered in the window.

My grandmother was sprawled on the floor, her legs crumpled beneath her.

"Nana Philly!" I cried, and dropped the laundry, running into the house.

Her eyes were wide, and there was a terrible bruise on the side of her face from where she had fallen.

"Avery! Help!" I shouted.

Nana Philly's mouth opened, but nothing came out.

Turned out that Nana Philly had had some kind of fit. Dr. Clarke called it a stroke. In the blink of an eye, everything had changed. An ant could run over her and she couldn't stop it.

All the cousins had been taking turns watching her. It was Ma's turn tonight. She had taken Buddy with her and left me in charge of Kermit here.

The house was quiet except for the buzzing of mosquitoes. They were thicker than ever. I had bites up and down my arms.

"Did Nana Philly say anything today?" Kermit asked.

I'd gone by to visit her this afternoon, but she hadn't seemed to know I was there.

"Nope, not one word," I said.

"Gosh. Do you think God punished her because she was so mean?"

"I think she's just old," I told my brother. But the truth was that I wondered about this myself.

The fire bell started ringing.

"Fire bell, Beans!" Kermit said.

It rang and rang and rang.

"Do you think it's a prank again?" Kermit asked.

"Stay here," I told him. "I want to see what's going on."

I went downstairs and stepped onto the porch. The night smelled like gardenia. But beneath the heady perfume, there was another faint scent. Something that tickled at my nose.

Smoke.

I followed the smell down the dark streets, and when I saw where the smoke was coming from, I felt like puking. I rubbed my eyes because I didn't want it to be true.

Smoke was pouring out of the Soldanos' place!

Mrs. Soldano was out front, shouting. I ran up to her.

"Where are the firemen?" I asked.

She looked bewildered. "They haven't come! I don't know why!"

But I did. Probably because they thought it was some rotten kid pulling a prank on them.

I took off running in my pajamas, through the dark alleys, faster than I've ever run in my life. When I reached the firehouse, I banged on the door.

Cem opened it.

"Shouldn't you be in bed, Beans?" he asked me, taking in my pajamas. Behind him, the other firemen were sitting around the table with their dominoes.

"There's a fire," I gasped. "On Ashe Street!"

They didn't get up.

One of the other men waved his hand. "Pfft. It's just a prank."

I grabbed Cem's arm. "You gotta believe me! I was just there! It's burning! The Soldanos'!"

Something in Cem's face shifted, and his eyes met mine.

"Game's over!" he barked. "Get the wagon!"

I rode with the firemen as the engine barreled down the street. The ride should have been exciting, but all I felt was sick. It was chaos when we reached Ashe

Street. Residents were screaming and crying and carrying everything they owned to the safest place: the cemetery, which had no houses and almost no trees to catch fire.

At Pork Chop's house, the Soldanos' belongings had been tossed into a pile on the street. It looked like it was everything they could rescue. Shoes and pictures and pillows. Chairs and a sofa. The kitchen table and a dresser. Pork Chop was picking things up.

"Pork Chop!" I called.

"Beans!" he shouted, and tossed a quilt into my arms. "Take it to the cemetery!"

"Gimme more!" I told him.

He gave me a pillow, his mother's knitting basket, and his father's suspenders. Arms full, we ran to the cemetery. We dumped everything and headed back for more.

Then came curtains, a rag rug, Mrs. Soldano's white slips, sheets, and a small, worn stuffed bear that I knew was my best pal's.

In no time at all, the cemetery had been transformed. It was littered with belongings: brass beds, chairs, kitchen tables, pots and pans, cribs, and piles of clothes. Even a piano had been wheeled over. The cemetery looked as if the living had taken up residence.

That night, as firemen fought the flames, lots of people slept there.

I was the only one who wished I was dead.

HIP, HIP, HOORAY

The fire was all anybody could talk about the next day at school. Even the teachers were gossiping about it.

"Such a tragedy," Miss Sugarapple murmured to another teacher in the hallway.

But Pork Chop wasn't there to hear it. He was absent.

"Mosquitoes started the fire," Ira announced at lunchtime. A bunch of kids had gathered around, listening.

"What?" I asked.

"My pa talked to Mr. Soldano. Mrs. Soldano was

burning a bunch of rags in kerosene to clear out the mosquitoes."

I remembered how thick they were last night.

"Guess she wasn't paying attention and the smudge pot tipped over. Next thing they knew, the kitchen was on fire."

Ashe Street had almost been taken out because of mosquitoes? Unbelievable.

I went by the Soldanos' place after school.

The smell of smoke still lingered in the air. The firemen had managed to keep the fire from spreading to the houses around the Soldanos'. But Pork Chop's place was a different story. No one would be coming to buy bolita numbers anytime soon.

The porch was badly burned, and the house's windows had shattered. There was glass everywhere. The smell was the worst. It stuck in your nose—a horrible combination of damp and smoke, worse than any garbage pile I'd ever climbed through.

Pork Chop sat across from his house, staring at it. He looked devastated.

"You okay, palsy?" I asked him.

"The phone melted," he said, a hollow look in his eyes.

"It did?"

He nodded.

After that day, I didn't ask if he was okay again. I already knew the answer.

Pork Chop and his family moved into his granny's house on Havana Lane. They didn't have the dough to fix their own place up.

"Mighty Mibsters challenged us again," Ira told us as we sat around Pork Chop's granny's kitchen, picking at food.

Mrs. Soldano's bollos didn't taste quite the same, for some reason. Maybe because she wasn't happy making them here under the watchful eyes of her mother-in-law. Pork Chop's granny was old and sat on a stool in a corner and stared at everyone.

This place was nothing like Mrs. Soldano's kitchen. It was quiet. No people coming and going. I missed the ringing phone most of all.

"Who cares," Pork Chop said, tugging at the collar of his shirt.

The shirt had been mended so many times that it was almost see-through. It was the only shirt he wore these days.

In school, they had taken up a collection of donated clothes for him and his family. But Pork Chop refused to wear any of them. Swore he'd rather go naked than wear some other kid's rags. He was gloomy now; he didn't have his usual snappy comebacks.

I tried to cheer things up.

"Come on, palsy. Let's play 'em," I said, forcing myself to grin. "It'll be a hoot to take their marbles."

His lips thinned. "Fine."

But it wasn't a hoot, because we played badly. Pork Chop didn't have his usual edge, and I overshot. Even Ira dragged his knuckles.

We lost. Twice.

The Keepsies were no longer on top of the marble game.

I knew it was all because of me.

The sword fell the next day at supper.

My mother turned to me and said, "Beans. You need to go down to Station Number Three."

I closed my eyes. Looked like my execution would be at the firehouse.

It was time to face the music.

As I followed my mother down the lane, I felt

like a criminal. Like Jelly. I wondered: Did they lock kids in jail? Would they let me out to come home for supper?

There was a small crowd gathered outside Fire Station No. 3 when we arrived, including Mr. and Mrs. Soldano, Pork Chop, Ira, Too Bad, and even Winky.

My humiliation was complete.

Inside the firehouse, the firemen were all standing around, looking grave. I could barely meet Cem's eyes.

"Beans," he said, stepping forward. "Thank you for coming."

My head snapped up. What was going on? Why was he thanking me instead of clapping irons on my arms?

"You are a shining example of bravery and integrity."

My mouth dropped open.

"If you had not come and fetched us, many more houses would have been lost." He paused. "You are a true hero in our community."

Then he held out a key that hung from a ribbon.

"This," he said, "is an honorary fire alarm key. May you be ever vigilant!"

I couldn't believe it. He'd just given *me* a key to the

fire alarms. All I could think was that Johnny Cakes would be thrilled.

He turned and shouted to the crowd, "Let's give Beans a *hip, hip, hooray!*"

Everyone shouted, "Hip, hip, hooray for Beans!"

Then people were congratulating me and slapping me on the back. The radio was turned up loud. Cuban music started playing, and someone brought out snacks. It was an impromptu celebration, and I was the guest of honor.

One by one, people came up to compliment me. Winky pushed his way through the crowd and slapped me on the back.

"I hear that my favorite worker saved the day!" he said. "How's it feel to be a hero?"

"'Scuse me," I said, and fought my way outside. I walked behind the firehouse.

And threw up.

HERO

All of Key West thought I was a hero.

Everywhere I went, people sang my praises. Even Miss Sugarapple was impressed. She let me lead the Pledge of Allegiance for the class and gave me thick slices of icebox cake from her own lunch.

That was just the beginning of free treats. Mrs. Albury dropped off tins of divinity. At Pepe's Café, they gave me all the Cuban ham sandwiches I could eat. And I got free ice cream for me and the whole gang at El Anon.

Me and the gang were sitting on one of the new

benches on Duval Street, having some of the cold treat.

"You need to be a hero more often, Beans," Ira said, taking a lick.

But my coconut ice cream tasted like sawdust in my mouth.

A bunch of kids walked by, and I heard them talking about me. But this time, they weren't talking about my marble skills.

"That's Beans Curry!"

One little kid broke away from the pack. He ran up to me. He couldn't have been more than five.

"Can I shake your hand?" the kid asked shyly.

"Why?" I said.

"'Cause my daddy says you're a real-life hero! He says I need to grow up just like you!"

But the worst part of it was how my mother reacted. She couldn't stop beaming.

"I'm just so proud of you, Beans!" she would say at odd moments.

If she only knew.

Then the nightmares started.

In my dreams, the air was full of smoke and the

sound of the fire bell ringing. I found myself waking up during the night and running downstairs to smell the night air. I was so tired that I walked around in a daze.

My stomach hurt. The guilt was eating away at me. I didn't know what to do and found myself walking to the most unlikely place: Nana Philly's house.

My cousin Miss Bea, a cheery older lady with silver hair, greeted me at the door.

"Why, Beans! So nice to see you!" she exclaimed.

Miss Bea had moved in and was taking care of Nana Philly. She must have been part angel to take care of the cranky old lady.

"How's she doing?" I asked.

"Oh, Philomena has her good days and her bad days. But she'll be so excited to see you!" she enthused. "She just loves her grandchildren."

Nana Philly was sitting up in a tufted chair in the parlor. It looked like she'd lost weight. She was wearing a nightgown and had a blanket tucked around her waist, and she was staring straight ahead.

At nothing.

"Beans," Miss Bea said, "I have to run down to the market. Can you sit with her for a little bit?"

"Sure," I said.

The door slammed and Miss Bea was gone, leaving me and Nana Philly all by ourselves.

"How ya feeling, Nana Philly?" I asked her.

She didn't say anything. Not that I expected her to. The doctor said she'd probably never be able to talk again.

I wished more than anything that she could yell at me. That *someone* would yell at me and tell me what a bad kid I was.

We sat there in silence. My gaze drifted to a little table with pictures. There was a photo of Ma as a young woman. She was beautiful, with a light in her eye, like she wanted to take on the world.

What would happen to that light if I came clean and told the truth? Fessed up to my part in the fire? Would she still be proud of me? Or would it make things even worse? Would people shun me? Shun the whole family? Would my family have to hide me away like a leper?

My head spun.

"I did something bad," I blurted out.

Nana Philly didn't blink.

Once I started, I couldn't seem to stop talking.

Words spilled from my mouth. "It was really bad. I didn't mean for it to happen. I was trying to help everyone."

I swallowed.

"Now I don't know what to do! I don't know if it would be worse if I told the truth or not!"

Then I covered my face with my hands, ashamed.

"What should I do? Should I tell the truth?" I pleaded.

She blinked.

"Does that blink mean yes or no?"

She blinked again. This was frustrating.

"Blink once for yes and two for no," I said.

She stared at me for a long moment and then blinked. Twice.

Well, what did I expect? She was the meanest woman in Key West. But she was also my grandmother. I knew she loved me. Just a little.

"I have one more question," I told her.

I swear she almost rolled her eyes.

"Did you try to kill Kermit with that potion for his throat?"

She blinked.

Once.

• • •

That night, I went to the late show at the movie theater. A comedy called *The Old-Fashioned Way* was playing. It starred Baby LeRoy and W. C. Fields. The baby even got top billing.

I sat in the balcony, half hoping that the leper man would be there. Maybe I could ask his opinion on things. Because despite my visit with Nana Philly, I didn't feel any better. If anything, I felt worse.

But then someone else slipped into the seat next to mine.

Dot.

"I hear you're a hero now," she said.

I didn't answer her.

Then the picture started rolling. On the screen, W. C. Fields and Baby LeRoy were yukking it up. I should have been excited. This was my kind of picture. But all I felt was sick inside. Next to me, Dot burst out laughing. But I couldn't laugh. I didn't deserve to be happy. I didn't deserve anything. Because I wasn't a hero. I was worse than any worst grown-up.

I was the lyingest liar in the whole world.

Something burst inside of me, and silent tears started rolling down my cheeks.

"I just love that baby, don't you?" Dot whispered to me, not looking away from the screen.

I couldn't answer; I was too busy crying.

"He's so funny! Isn't he a hoot? Don't you . . ." And then her voice trailed off as she looked at me. Her eyes widened.

"Beans," she whispered. "You okay?"

I hated her more in that moment than any other. I wished she would just go away and let me cry in peace in the dark theater. I couldn't take it anymore; I couldn't breathe. I wished I could just disappear—

Then Dot's hand slipped into mine.

And squeezed.

I held on tight until the last credit rolled.

DOOMED

A few days later, I ran into the last person in the world I wanted to see: Johnny Cakes.

I was out walking with Little Dizzy. He was asleep in the wagon, Termite waddling after us. Mrs. Albury had asked me to babysit him in return for divinity. I couldn't say no to her divinity.

Johnny Cakes was strolling down White Street toward the docks.

"There you are," he said with a grin. "I've been look-ing for you. I have a job."

"No, thanks."

He looked surprised. "I'll pay you double."

For a brief moment I was tempted, but then I remembered the smell of smoke.

I shook my head.

He frowned. "I'm sorry to hear that. You were a good employee."

I was *too* good of an employee.

"I gotta go," I said. "The baby wakes up if I stand still too long."

"If you change your mind . . ."

"I won't," I said firmly.

I walked away.

The next day at school, just as recess was ending, a kid came running up to me, calling my name.

"Beans! Beans!"

I didn't bother to look back. The last thing I needed was some kid praising me for being a hero.

"It's your dog!" the kid shouted.

That got my attention.

I froze, then turned around. "My dog?"

"Yeah!" the kid said. "The dogcatchers just got him! He was right outside the school. I saw it with my own two eyes!"

Pork Chop asked me, "You think they'll kill him?"

Could things possibly get any worse? Wasn't it bad enough that my life was ruined? And now my dog's was, too?

That afternoon at school was the longest ever. The minute the bell rang, me and Pork Chop and Ira headed downtown to where the New Dealers had set up shop.

The office used to be a vacant storefront. Now it was buzzing with activity. There was a big sign announcing: VOLUNTEERS WANTED. I followed the sound of barking dogs to the back of the building, where cages were lined up. I saw four skinny hounds and one short, funny-looking one.

"There he is!" Ira said.

My dog barked happily.

"Termite," I said to him.

A man who had slicked-back hair and wore Bermuda shorts came around the back, carrying a bowl of water.

"'Scuse me, mister," I said. "That's my dog in there."

"Which one?" he asked.

"The short, funny-looking one. Please, can I have him back?" I pleaded.

"Well—" the man began.

Pork Chop interrupted. "Beans sure does love his dog, mister."

The man narrowed his eyes at me. "You're Beans? The kid who helped with the firemen?"

I nodded reluctantly.

The man gave me a once-over. "I heard about you. You did a good thing." He glanced at the cage. "Go on, you can take him."

As we walked down the street, I looked back at the man in Bermuda shorts.

"I'd keep him tied up or inside if I was you," he warned me.

"Thanks, mister," I said.

Maybe the New Dealers weren't so bad after all.

I still had a dime left from the Johnny Cakes money, and there was a new picture playing at the movie theater.

It was called *Little Friend* and starred a newcomer kid actress named Nova Pilbeam. She'd have to be pretty good to get anywhere with that name.

This time when I went to the balcony, the leper was there. He didn't seem all that surprised to see me. I sat right next to him. We were the only ones there.

"I hear this picture is good," he said. "Supposed to be very dramatic."

I'd heard the same thing.

"What's your name?" I asked him.

"Murray," he said. "What's yours?"

"Beans."

He tilted his head. "Is there a story behind that nickname?"

"From when I was a baby. Ma said every time she nursed me after she ate beans, I'd toot all night long. So she started calling me Beans."

He chuckled.

We watched the picture and, boy, was it ever dramatic. It was about a girl whose parents were getting divorced. It was sad as can be. I didn't like it one bit. Give me a comedy any day.

Afterward, me and Murray walked home together through the dark lanes. As we passed one of the little Conch houses, Murray paused, studying it.

"What color is it?" he asked me.

"What?"

"The house. I can tell it's been painted, but I can't see the color in the dark."

"The New Dealers painted it pink."

"That's an interesting choice," he said.

"You said it."

As we walked, Murray pointed out other changes the New Dealers had made. Weeds had been cut back to showcase red-blooming poinciana trees. Porches that were hidden before now looked inviting. The garbage was gone. I started to see everything with new eyes.

But it was the air that was so different—it didn't stink. Instead, it smelled of frangipani and the tangy bite of the ocean. The island's own perfume. It smelled good and fresh and alive.

That's when I knew.

I couldn't fix the damage done to the Soldanos' house. But maybe I could fix something else.

The next day after school, I went to the New Dealers' office. The same fella who had given me back Termite was manning the front desk.

"Did you lose your dog again?"

"I'm here to volunteer," I said.

"We don't take kids," the man said.

"Why not?" I asked. "I can help!"

"Sorry."

"Look, I'll do whatever you ask!" I told him desperately. "I've worked dirty jobs before. I'm not afraid of hard work."

He leaned back in his chair and studied me.

"Did you say you don't mind doing dirty jobs?"

"I'll do anything, mister. Just tell me."

I was cleaning outhouses by the end of the day.

I did every dirty job there was: I cleaned outhouses and strained bugs out of cisterns. I filled in potholes and shoveled up trash from vacant lots. I went home filthy and tired every day, but with a lighter heart.

"Were you collecting milk cans again?" my mother asked me one evening when I came home stinking like a dead animal. I'd spent the afternoon picking up trash along Duval Street. I was a big fan of garbage cans these days.

"I was helping the New Dealers," I told her.

She looked surprised. "Really?"

I nodded.

"You've always been a good boy," she said.

Not always. Not by a long shot. But maybe there was still hope.

One night after supper, I realized I had brought a shovel home from the office. When I went to take it back, the light was still on. I peeked inside.

The head lunatic himself was sitting alone at a desk.

"I'm just bringing back the shovel," I told him.

"Thank you, Peas."

"Beans," I said.

"Of course," he said distractedly. "I noticed that none of you children are using the playground."

It was the truth.

"If I can't get children to play on a playground, how am I possibly going to turn around this city?" He sounded defeated.

"It might just take a while," I told him.

"We don't have a while! It's already November. We only have a few weeks left until the opening of tourist season, and there's still so much to be done. Nobody seems to understand the gravity of the situation. If Key West is not ready for business by this tourist season, it's doomed."

"What do you mean, *doomed?*"

He put his hands on his forehead and rubbed. "They're already discussing it in Washington! It would cost less money to close down Key West and move its citizens somewhere else than to try to save it."

I couldn't believe it.

"But they can't do that! This is our home!"

"They can and they will." He sighed heavily. "At this point, it will take a genuine miracle to save this town."

DIVINE DIVINITY

I sat on the seesaw in the empty playground.

It was squally out, the sky gray, the way it always got before a bad storm. All around town, folks went about their business, unconcerned. Nobody had any idea of the storm that was headed our way if tourists didn't show up.

I looked around the playground. Maybe I could try to get some kids to play there. Set up a marble tournament or something.

But the more I thought about it, the more I didn't see how that would help, really. Like Mr. Stone said, there was still a lot of work to be done to get ready for the tourists.

Mr. Stone was going about it all wrong, I realized.

He didn't need us kids on this playground.

He needed *us kids.*

"You want us to do *what?*" Pork Chop asked me in bewilderment.

"We need to get kids to help out the New Dealers!"

He made a face. "You're all wet!"

"You know," Ira said, studying me, "you've been real strange since the whole fire thing. Is being a hero going to your head?"

"Come on, fellas," I said. "I'm serious. Mr. Stone told me they might close Key West down."

"Baloney! They can't close down a town," Pork Chop said with a scowl.

"They can do anything they want," I replied.

Pork Chop looked at Ira, who nodded his head.

"Fine, we'll help," Pork Chop agreed. "I still think it's a bunch of applesauce."

We spent the whole afternoon talking to kids from one side of town to the other. Most kids heard me out. But by the end of the day, all we had was one volunteer.

Too Bad.

"Ready to work, Boss!" he said with a snappy salute.

Now we were really doomed.

That night, I sat in Kermit's room, keeping him company and eating Mrs. Albury's divinity. I flipped through some Hollywood magazines that Murray had let me borrow.

Kids were sure getting a lot of publicity these days. There were articles on Shirley Temple and Jackie Cooper. There was also a two-page spread of Hollywood actors modeling Bermuda shorts. Looked like they were the latest fashion after all.

Kermit picked up a piece of divinity and studied it. Then he put it down and picked up another.

"Just take one already!" I told him.

"But it's so good that it's hard to pick a piece!" Kermit said, licking his fingers. "I'd do anything for this divinity."

I looked up from my magazine. "What did you say?"

"I said I'd do anything for this divinity."

"That's it!" I said.

Maybe we didn't need a miracle to save Key West.

Maybe all we needed was divinity.

I was going to bribe every kid in Key West with Mrs. Albury's divinity.

The next day, we spread the word at school. Any kid who volunteered to help Mr. Stone would get divinity. I gave out free samples to build excitement By the end of the day, I had dozens of boys lined up and ready to work.

Then something unexpected happened.

Dot showed up. With a whole gang of girls. There must have been thirty of them.

"I hear you've got divinity," she said.

We went down to the New Dealers' office after school. The kids waited outside while I went in.

"Can I see Mr. Stone?" I asked the fella at the front desk. He was the one who had let me take Termite home. His name was Tommy, and I'd gotten to know him a little from volunteering. He was from New York City and liked to talk about it. How there were tall skyscrapers and that the city lit up at night. I kind of wanted to see it someday.

"He's in a meeting, Beans," Tommy told me.

"Tell him it's important," I said.

Tommy gave me a long look and then went into a back room. A moment later, Mr. Stone walked out, looking surprised.

"What can I do for you, Peas?"

I opened the door and pointed. Dozens and dozens of kids with bare feet and patched-up clothes stood in the street.

"What can *we* do for *you?*" I replied.

Mr. Stone put us to work.

We kids started to do everything the grown-ups were doing and more. We painted benches and fences. We pulled weeds and planted flowers.

Then there was the seaweed. Clumps of rotting, smelly seaweed littered the beach that the tourists were going to use. It attracted buzzing flies. Mr. Stone gave us kids the job of shoveling it up. Talk about dirty work.

"This is ridiculous," Pork Chop said as we tossed a pile of seaweed into a wheelbarrow. "It's just gonna wash back up again in the next good storm."

But I gave him a piece of divinity, and the sweet candy melted his crankiness right away.

Word spread, and soon it felt like nearly every kid on the island was volunteering.

I broke the news to Mrs. Albury.

"We're gonna need a *lot* more divinity," I told her.

All around, there was a new energy. Folks were pitching in to transform Conch Town into a Hollywood picture. Rustic thatched-roof cabanas were built on Rest Beach. A hospitality league was formed. Fishermen were encouraged to clean up their boats to take tourists out fishing.

It was my enterprising idea to make souvenirs to sell to the tourists. I had kids collect shells, and we glued them on wooden cigar boxes that I got Johnny Cakes to donate. He wasn't all that bad for a criminal.

It seemed like everybody was trying to help.

And I do mean *everybody*.

Late one night, I saw Murray and a few other folks who looked like they had leprosy planting flowers along Duval Street.

"What are you doing?" I asked him.

"Heard you kids were helping out," he said with a shrug. "Our fingers may be falling off, but we're not useless."

I wondered if his fingers really were falling off, but I decided not to ask.

Besides, there was no time for questions. Everyone was too busy trying to make Key West shine like a new penny. It felt like we were making a Hollywood movie. We wanted applause. We wanted good reviews. We wanted our name in lights.

Before we knew it, it was opening night for our town.

The film was in the projector. The theater went dark. The curtain was raised.

We held our breath as the picture started rolling.

OPENING NIGHT

They came in their Bermuda shorts and smart linen dresses and shiny shoes.

They strolled down Duval and filled up the rooms at the newly opened, plush Casa Marina Hotel. They ventured onto the little lanes, eager to see our island. They arrived by boat and train and automobile.

We had been invaded again.

By tourists.

"Here comes two more!" Pork Chop hissed.

A sign that said SOLDANO'S announced the little lunch

counter set under the porch in front of Pork Chop's house. The Soldanos' place had been fixed courtesy of New Dealer money. Mr. Stone thought it was important to have "local color," so I convinced him to build Mrs. Soldano a lunch counter where she could serve authentic Cuban cuisine to the tourists. And, of course, he would fix up the damage from the fire in the process.

"Hello, ma'am! Hello, sir!" I greeted the tourists. "Would you like to try some delicious Cuban cuisine?"

The lady was wearing big sunglasses, a wide hat, and a pretty striped dress. She looked like she'd stepped out of a Hollywood movie.

"Oh, darling, would you look at that?" she said to the man.

"Are you kids the welcoming committee?" he asked with a smile.

"We sure are!" Too Bad said with a grin.

"How charming," she declared. "We'd love to."

They sat down on stools and surveyed the menu.

"What do you suggest?" the man asked Mrs. Soldano.

"I just finished a batch of bollos," she said.

My best pal's mom was back to her usual self, cooking away. Of course, she still sold bolita numbers out of her kitchen. Nobody could stop bolita.

Or booze. I heard that Johnny Cakes couldn't bring in the liquor fast enough for the thirsty tourists.

Avery was busy, too.

I ran into him later that day. He had his easel set up by the ocean. His paintings, and those of the other New Dealer artists, now hung in cafés and bars all around town.

"So what do you think?" he asked.

I studied the picture he was painting: tourists in swimsuits, lounging on the beach.

"To be honest, it's not as good as your houses."

He chuckled. "I meant Key West. It seems Mr. Stone's little experiment might be working out. There sure are a lot of tourists."

"Can't walk down a lane without tripping on one," I said. "Worse than termites."

"Say, I'm going to give art lessons. Would you like to come?"

"Sure," I said. "Maybe I can give *you* some tips."

We both laughed.

It seemed our little town was becoming especially popular with the artist crowd. Murray swore that Hollywood actors were visiting Key West.

"I heard that Myrna Loy checked into the Casa Marina last night!" he told me. For a guy who only came out at night, he certainly knew what was what.

But it wasn't just actors. Painters and writers were showing up in droves. I was in the New Dealer office when one of them walked in.

"The hotel's full up," the man said. "I'm looking for accommodations."

"What's your name, mister?" I asked him.

"Robert Frost."

"What do you do?"

"I'm a poet."

"Hey, we got a writer living here," I told him. Then I lowered my voice. "He's not very good, though."

"Really?" the man asked curiously. "What's his name?"

"Ernest Hemingway."

Then someone more exciting than any Hollywood actor or fancy author arrived in Key West.

When I got home from school one afternoon, my father's shoes were sitting on the front porch.

"Poppy!" I cried when I opened the door.

He was sitting at the little kitchen table.

"Have you grown?" he asked me with a fond smile.

166

"Yes," I told him.

Because I had.

"Tell Beans the news," my mother said.

"I got a job," he announced.

My stomach twisted a little.

"In New Jersey?"

He shook his head. "Matecumbe Key. On the highway."

Matecumbe was a little key north of Key West.

"I'll work up there during the week and come back on the weekends," he said. "How does that sound to you?"

It sounded wonderful, like a Hollywood movie.

I half expected Shirley Temple to tap-dance through our kitchen.

Me and the gang were sitting in front of the New Dealer office with a wagon full of babies.

We had Dizzy and Clara today. Little Clara was the baby of a couple vacationing in Key West. Ma did their laundry, so I had offered to watch the baby. What was one more baby, after all?

"Say, there's gonna be a game of marbles after lunch," Ira announced.

"Who's playing?" I asked.

"Mighty Mibsters," Ira said.

"Sure," I said. "Always happy to take the Mibsters' marbles."

Pork Chop grinned at me. "You shred it, wheat!"

The Keepsies were back on top. We hadn't lost a game in weeks. Nobody could touch us.

A man in a suit and a fedora walked up to us.

"Hello there, kids," the man said. "I'm a newspaperman from New York City, here to do a feature about the Key West story."

"The Key West story?" It kind of sounded like a movie title.

"Folks are calling this place Recovery Key because you've managed to turn things around. It's heartwarming. People can't get enough of it." He looked closely at me. "What's your name?"

"Beans Curry."

"You grow up here?"

"Sure did. I'm a Key West Conch."

He gestured to the wagon of sleeping babies.

"So, you offer a babysitting service for visiting tourists?" he asked.

"I guess so."

"Beans has a way with babies!" Kermit said.

"*A way with babies.* I *like* it!" the newspaperman said, writing down the quote. "What a smart little business-man you are. Even mothers need a vacation."

I felt like I had been struck by lightning. That was it! It was the perfect business idea, and it had been in front of my eyes the entire time.

We would peddle babies.

"Can I snap a photo of you and your gang of kids?" the man asked us.

"Why not?" I said.

We posed in front of the New Dealer office, our feet dirty and bare for the whole world to see.

"What should I call you in the caption?" he asked.

I smiled. "The Diaper Gang."

DIAPER GANG

It was June and steamy as the inside of an automobile engine. Tourist season was over and Key West was sleepy again.

"My cousin in Ohio wrote that he saw the newspaper article you were interviewed for," Ira said to me.

Me and Ira and Pork Chop were walking down Duval Street, pulling a wagon full of babies. We had three tykes packed tight into the wagon like sausages.

"Really?" I asked.

"He said you're famous!" Ira nodded, his corkscrew

curls bouncing. "He wrote that every kid knows about Beans Curry and the Diaper Gang."

That sounded good to me.

"Maybe I'll get a screen test with Warner Brothers after all," I mused.

I didn't know if I would be discovered, but Key West certainly had been. The Casa Marina was already booked up for the next season. Mr. Stone and his band of merry New Dealers were planning more improvements. He wanted to put on theater shows and art gallery exhibits. He was bringing in more artists to paint murals around town and was even importing bicycles for the tourists.

The changes were apparent everywhere. More restaurants had opened. Stores, too. The lingering despair had disappeared with the piles of garbage. Everybody was happier these days.

A wailing came from the wagon.

Well, *almost* everybody was happier.

"I swear, Pudding's the worst," Pork Chop muttered, shaking his head at the squalling baby. The other two babies were fast asleep like little angels dropped from heaven.

Pudding was a bad baby. Kid never stopped crying. I blamed his mother. She always picked him up. If I'd learned anything, it was that you had to let a baby be.

Ira pointed down the street. "At least Pudding ain't as bad as him!"

Heading our way was Winky.

"Beans!" Winky called with a fake smile. "How ya doing, palsy?"

Pork Chop rolled his eyes.

"Nice day, huh, boys?" Winky said.

"Whaddya want, Winky?" I asked.

Just 'cause I pulled babies around didn't mean I was soft. In fact, I was harder than ever.

"I was just wondering if you'd be interested in working for me again."

"Nope."

"I'll give you a dime for twenty cans," he wheedled.

"Can't help you, Winky," I told him.

"You won't even have to clean the cans!" he cajoled. "I'll do that part!"

"Sorry," I replied.

Babies were big business. The Diaper Gang had a waiting list for our wagon. Every mother in town was dying to know my secret formula for diaper rash. I even made up rules for the gang. The first rule was: no girls allowed.

I liked being my own boss. It didn't even bother me that most of the mothers paid us in homemade candy. It always tasted sweet, and it was a lot less complicated than money.

"But, Beans!" Winky pleaded.

I ignored him and turned to Pork Chop.

"Come on," I said. "We got babies."

"Pos-i-tute-ly!" Pork Chop agreed.

We left Winky standing in the dust.

We pulled the wagon past the movie theater. Murray was getting me into the late show for free these days because of his cousin. We'd seen the latest Shirley Temple picture a few nights ago. She was a genuine star now.

But some things never changed.

Mr. Stone was striding down the street in his underwear. I mean, his Bermuda shorts.

"Why, Peas! How nice to see you," Mr. Stone said.

I didn't bother to correct him anymore. I was kind of used to him calling me Peas.

"Here, take a stack of these and drop them off as you go around town," he told us, shoving a pile of brochures into my hand.

Pork Chop peered over my shoulder.

"'Hospitality Hints for the Key West Resident'?" he read.

Mr. Stone looked enthusiastic. "It's just some tips to make our little island welcoming for the tourists."

I flipped through it. The hints included *Be friendly to visitors*, *Keep Key West as quiet as possible*, and *Do not soak the tourists*.

Hmmm. Now that the city was cleaned up, Mr. Stone was apparently trying to renovate its inhabitants.

"And look," he pointed out helpfully. "It suggests that parents encourage children to play in the playground. You have been using the playground, haven't you?"

"Yes, sir, Mr. Stone. We use that playground every single day. From morning to night," I assured him, even though no one used it.

"That's wonderful to hear! Keep up the good work!" he said. "I mean, keep up the good *play!*"

Pudding started fussing again.

"Gotta go," I told Mr. Stone.

174

As we walked away, Pork Chop snorted. "Laid it on a bit thick, didn't ya?"

"Easier to just tell grown-ups what they want to hear," I said.

Because it was. I told every mother whose tot I watched that her child was the best baby in town.

"Say," Ira said. "I hear there's a new marble crew in town. They're calling themselves the Amazing Aggies."

"Amazing Aggies? That's a pretty good name," I admitted.

"They're playing the Mighty Mibsters later this morning," Ira added.

I wasn't all that concerned. The Keepsies were still the best marble crew in town. Every kid wanted to be in our gang. Not that we wanted them all.

"Hey, Beans!" Too Bad called. "You fellas need any help?"

Kid was still like a flea.

"No way, no how, Too Bad," Pork Chop said, waving him away.

I leaned down and gave the wailing Pudding a sniff. The baby had a full diaper and, boy, do I mean *full*.

"Let the kid have a try changing the diaper," I said.

Pork Chop looked at me like I was a lunatic.

"If he can change the diaper, I'll think about letting him in the gang," I explained.

Too Bad looked thrilled. "Maybe I can get a new nickname, too?"

"We'll see," I said, and slapped a clean cloth diaper in his outstretched hand.

"Show us what you got," I told him, stepping back to observe.

Too Bad laid a blanket on the ground and lifted the squalling Pudding out of the wagon. He slipped the clean diaper under the baby's bungy with one hand before removing the soiled diaper with the other. That was my trick, too. Kept the blanket clean.

But before Too Bad could continue, Pudding let out an enormous toot. Too Bad was so startled that his hand holding the soiled diaper flew out.

And landed on my chest with a wet splat.

"Too Bad!" I barked.

The kid gasped in horror. "I'm real sorry, Beans! Honest!"

I shook my head. Maybe I was the one who needed a new nickname.

Too Stupid seemed about right.

• • •

After we returned the babies to the loving arms of their mothers, I settled on the swing in the cool shade of the front porch to enjoy my candy. Poppy's shoes weren't on the porch, but it was all right. He came home most weekends.

From inside the house, a voice protested loudly.

"I don't wanna take a nap!"

These days, it wasn't Buddy who was trying to get out of naps. It was Kermit.

I heard Ma shout in frustration, "Do you want to die? Is that what you want?"

Kermit wasn't confined to his bed anymore. But the doctor insisted that he take a nap every day because of his heart.

Termite growled and I looked up. A figure was strolling up the lane.

Dot.

"Beans," she said shortly.

"Dot," I replied. "Whaddya want?"

"I thought you'd want to know that we just beat the Mighty Mibsters."

That made me sit up. "Who's 'we'?"

"Didn't you hear? I've got my own marble crew now. All girls. The Amazing Aggies."

Then she grinned.

"Just let me know when you want us to beat you boys," she said as she strolled off.

I still hated that girl.

No sooner had Dot disappeared than I heard the rumble of a car. It was an old Ford Model A, nothing like the slick Ford Model 730 Deluxe V-8 sedan. The two people getting out of it didn't resemble Bonnie and Clyde one bit: they were a middle-aged man with a pot-belly and a young girl carrying a mangy cat.

"Excuse me, son," the man called to me.

Judging by his rumpled suit, he was a salesman. He looked greasy and slick. Something about him reminded me of Winky.

"What are you selling, mister?" I asked in a bored voice.

He brightened. "Well, since you asked, I do happen to have some Hair Today back in my automobile."

"What's it do?"

"Makes your hair grow," he said, pointing to his bald head. "It's guaranteed to work in one month or your money back."

Even a baby wouldn't fall for a scam like that.

I snorted. "Guess *you* ain't a satisfied customer."

As he sputtered, I shook my head. Grown-ups were such lying liars.

But then again, kids were, too.

The important thing was to watch out for the bad lies.

And never, *ever* get Winkied.

AUTHOR'S NOTE

At the height of the Great Depression, Key West was in dire straits. The majority of the inhabitants were unemployed and on public relief. Municipal services had become sporadic, including garbage collection. The town went bankrupt.

Garbage cleanup in Key West neighborhood

As part of President Franklin D. Roosevelt's New Deal, the management of the town was taken over by the Federal Emergency Relief Administration. The fate of Key West lay in the hands of Julius Stone, Jr., who had been appointed as administrator. Julius Stone saw two options: to abandon the town and relocate its inhabitants or to remake it as a tourist destination—"the Bermuda of Florida," as he called it. He chose the latter.

Stone's plan was met with suspicion by many locals, but also with enthusiasm. In the end, Key West citizens volunteered thousands of hours of time to rehabilitate their island. They cleaned lots, repaired streets, built park benches, renovated houses and hotels, repaired outdated plumbing, planted palm trees and flowers, and built cabanas and playgrounds and parks. Thousands of cubic yards of garbage were collected and trucked out. Even the island's children volunteered. They pulled weeds and painted fences and shoveled up seaweed.

Children raking seaweed off the beach to beautify it

In addition to the volunteers, Julius Stone brought in artists to help advertise Key West to the world. They painted idyllic posters, brochures, and postcards of Key West to lure visitors.

Cover of brochure produced to advertise
Key West as a tourist destination

Interior painting from brochure by artist
Edward Bruce illustrating "typical Key West lane"

And it worked.

An estimated forty thousand tourists came that first winter, and the "Key West Experiment" was deemed a success. The island became a winter destination, especially for writers, including the poet Robert Frost. "Recovery Key," as it came to be known, was one of the longest-lasting success stories of the New Deal.

Fire was a constant fear in Key West because of its wooden houses. The fire bell in the cemetery was an alert system for firemen as well as residents. The story of people taking their belongings to the cemetery to safeguard them from a fire was related to me by a cousin.

Key West Fire Department personnel
posing in front of Fire Station No. 3

Fire Station No. 3, at the corner of Grinnell and Virginia Streets, heroically stayed open during the worst of the Great Depression, when other firehouses closed. Today, it is the Key West Firehouse Museum, and you can visit it.

Kids started to become big business in Hollywood in the 1930s. Children got studio contracts and even merchandising deals, for everything from clothing lines to toys. The most notable "baby" performer was Baby LeRoy. But without doubt, it was newcomer Shirley Temple who captured the heart of a nation.

Child stars Baby LeRoy and Shirley Temple

The story of Murray and the lepers was inspired by Dorothy Raymor, who was a reporter for the *Key West Citizen*. In her book *Key West Collection* (The Ketch & Yawl Press, 1999), she quotes a local man telling her about the lepers living in Key West:

"If you should wander into the back sections of our movie balconies at night," Earle advised, "you might spot some of the 'Night People.' Some have disfigured faces and some are crippled and have lost fingers, toes and even limbs."

I was fascinated by this tidbit. I did more research and discovered an epidemiologist's report noting that 80 percent of the cases of leprosy in Florida were in Key West—and 60 percent of those afflicted lived in a five-block area.

Finally, while Pork Chop's colorful sayings were rooted in the time period, one phrase was supplied by my daughter. It has been commonplace in our household.

As Millie likes to say when she is startled or confused . . . *What in the history of cheese?*

BEANS'S FAVORITE KID ACTORS

Matthew "Stymie" Beard, *School's Out* (1930)

Jackie Cooper, *Treasure Island* (1934)

Junior Durkin, *Huckleberry Finn* (1931)

Bobby "Wheezer" Hutchins, *Mush and Milk* (1933)

Mary Ann Jackson, *Fly My Kite* (1931)

Baby LeRoy, *The Old-Fashioned Way* (1934)

George "Spanky" McFarland, *For Pete's Sake!* (1934)

Dickie Moore, *Forgotten Babies* (1933)

Shirley Temple, *Little Miss Marker* (1934)

Jane Withers, *Bright Eyes* (1934)

PORK CHOP'S BEST SAYINGS

Baloney!

Don't go having kittens!

For the love of Pete!

Mind your own potatoes!

Pos-i-tute-ly!

Tell it to Sweeney!

You shred it, wheat!

You're all wet!

What a bunch of applesauce!

What in the history of cheese?

OFFICIAL RULES
OF THE DIAPER GANG

1. No girls allowed.

2. Keep your rag clean.

3. Always duck when changing a diaper.

4. Don't tell the secret diaper-rash formula.

RESOURCES TO KEEP THE CONVERSATION GOING

Baby LeRoy:

imdb.com/name/nm0045128/

Florida and the New Deal:

fcit.usf.edu/florida/lessons/depress/depress1.htm

The Great Depression:

Pascal, Janet B. *What Was the Great Depression?*
New York: Grosset & Dunlap, 2015.

How to make old-fashioned divinity candy:

pastrysampler.com/Recipes/Confectionery
/Chocolate_Divinity.html

Key West Firehouse Museum:

keywestfirehousemuseum.com

Shirley Temple:

Kasson, John F. *The Little Girl Who Fought the
Great Depression: Shirley Temple and 1930s America.*
New York: W. W. Norton, 2014.

Works Progress Administration artists in Key West:

keysarts.com/public_art/wpa.html

ACKNOWLEDGMENTS

The recollections of my family members and other Conchs helped me bring to life the everyday details of Key West, and I am grateful to them all. I am especially indebted to Kurt and Monica Lewin, Annette Liggett, and Tom Hambright. I am also grateful for the Conchs who have passed away since I first interviewed them. Your memories live on.

In addition, I am grateful for the incredible support and enthusiasm from the whole gang at Random House, including Casey Lloyd, Mallory Loehr, Adrienne Waintraub, and Barbara Marcus. Thank you for championing my work. Special appreciation to Michelle Nagler, who encouraged my "oomph!"

Finally, I'd like to thank all the Dots in my life who held my hand on the balcony when I was feeling low—especially Kirby Larson, Shannon Hale, Jen Longo, Marc Tyler Nobleman, Jill Applebaum, and Jill Grinberg.

I would be honored to be in a gang with any of you.

ABOUT THE AUTHOR

JENNIFER L. HOLM is the *New York Times* best-selling children's author of *The Fourteenth Goldfish* and, with her brother Matthew Holm, *Sunny Side Up*. She is the recipient of three Newbery Honors for her novels *Our Only May Amelia, Penny from Heaven,* and *Turtle in Paradise.* Jennifer also collaborates with Matthew on three graphic novel series—the Eisner Award–winning Babymouse series, the bestselling Squish series, and My First Comics. Jennifer lives in California. You can visit her on the Web at jenniferholm.com.